Betting on Paradise

By
L. Wendell Vaughan

Grosbeak Books
New Bedford, MA
USA

Books by
L. Wendell Vaughan

Rabbits and Moons (Book 1)

Betting on Paradise (Book 2)

Library of Congress Control Number:
Library of Congress Cataloging-in-Publication Data
Vaughan, L. Wendell
Betting on Paradise: a novel/L..Wendell Vaughan **2nd edition**. Betting on Paradise has been re-edited since being published in 2023.

Betting on Paradise may be purchased for educational, business, or sales promotional use. For information please email: grosbeakbooks@gmail.com

Book cover design Grosbeak Books
Photograph by Meric-Dagli

ISBN 978-0-9702979-6-9 paperback
ISBN 978-0-9702979-7-6 hardcover
ISBN 978-0-9702979-8-3 digital ebook

To Paul
Thank you for listening

"Take the risk
or
lose the chance....."

Marko Halilovic

Chapter
1

Mexico City

A shoeshine boy, not more than five years old, greased and buffed Liam's *Santoni* penny loafers. The caramel color had become tarnished with travel, and it was imperative to Liam that they looked spotless for his meeting. The boy's hands were pudgy, his nails blackened by the dark wax. His bangs shrouded eyes that, when they appeared, looked glossy and their expression dull. With each slap of his cloth on the leather, he grunted. Sometimes he whistled an upbeat tune. It was as though the sounds were a form of entertainment, Liam thought, examining the holes and stains in the boy's clothing. It was early morning, and Liam's mood was suffering from the pressure of having to be in a city, he had no desire to be in. He was to assist his family with a matter he found stupid but possibly profitable. He said 'yes' because he was broke. After years of *...he couldn't quite remember all the details, but he was sure he'd been having fun,* his trust fund had been depleted to a few lackluster Chilean pesos. And now, being a little fuzzy from last night's bender, it all caused him to be reflective, and he wondered:

if he hadn't been born rich, would he, too, have spent his early years shining shoes? Repulsed by the idea, he shifted his weight from one cheek to the other, then arched an eyebrow. "Possibly I'd be a better man and would have learned the true value of a penny?" But this statement made him laugh. "How ludicrous!" The boy looked up, and Liam scowled at him.

Liam wore a tailored gray suit. His white shirt was unbuttoned at the neck, his tie in his jacket pocket. A tall, good-looking man in his early forties, he sat with knees arched and back flush against the wrought-iron seat. The expression on his well-formed face was perplexed, if not a touch tormented. Treading his eyes over the Bellas Artes Park, the sun bright, the birds singing, he had a cup of coffee in one hand and a pan dulce in the other. With every sip, the burn of the whiskey-infused beverage burned his throat, and with every sip, the guilt of still needing mummy and daddy's money dissipated. When memories of his nightly rendezvous fluttered in, they caused him to lick his fingers like a sugary pacifier. He had been out late. The exact recall blurred yet etched in his mind like a seedy porn movie. He had not been looking for the high tack area, but when the taxi driver from the airport took a shortcut to the Centro District by the infamous *linea de puta*, his evening plans became apparent. The girls, young and old, wearing stilettos, short skirts, and fluffy low-cut blouses, were irresistible. He bought three. *What a tasty night the world had provided*, he mused. He itched his crotch and gave a haughty growl at the scrumptious memory of brown nipples wiggling between his teeth.

Taking a bottle of antidepressants out of his pants pocket, he popped the top off with his teeth and put two onto his tongue. Head swung back, he swallowed. *That ought to do the trick* to *keep these fun thoughts fluid*. But for some reason he immediately fell into negativity. The air was clear and crisp, but in an hour, this city would become a sooty mess once the traffic picked up. *Mexico City was such a drag that way.* Liam preferred the Cape Town air in South Africa, the ocean breeze exquisite. Then the thought of home brought on images of his wife and child, and his outlook grew even more sullen. His wife was on the verge of getting what was left of his trust fund, the house, and his savings. He cursed himself for sleeping with his lawyer. For once he should have kept chaste. As it went, his lawyer caught him with his Zulu lover while investigating a matter in the township of Soweto, and that was that. Looking down at the shoeshine boy, he quipped, "Aren't you done yet? I can't be late, or I'll have to steal your shoeshine box. Yup, the last of my dough is this pathetic wad of pesos in my pocket." He eyed the lump and sighed.

Liam's Chilean accent confused the child, but he sensed enough to stop and nodded for his client to inspect the job. Liam examined his shoes and pointed out a few spots he had missed. The child shrugged and with his grimy, niblet fingers, he smeared a pinch of wax over a crease and began buffing again. Liam emptied the contents of his whiskey bottle into the coffee cup, lit a cigarette, took a mindless pull, and coughed. Phlegm retched from his lungs. The boy looked askew at the man and stopped again. Sitting back on his haunches, he placed the rag across his knee the way he had seen the older boys do and held out his hand to be paid.

Liam relaxed, the booze and drugs having collided, he pondered the youngster's small cherub face. It was such a mess and covered with what looked like days of crud around his mouth and cheeks. He dug into his pocket and gave the boy a few centavos, along with his leftover bread. "A tip," he said. The boy looked puzzled but took the bread and ate a bite, then picked up his shoeshine box and scooted away. The sight of his small body running off had Liam pondering whether there might be a sort of freedom in being poor, a certain lack of responsibility and judgment from one's peers. *But then every group had their rules and judgments*, he sighed feeling irked and flummoxed at the overall state of human behavior.

Tossing his empty cup into the bushes, he shrugged and walked off toward the Zócalo. His long strides were purposeful. His shoes clipped along the cement walkway sounding like a newly shod horse; his gray thin linen pants swayed with the matching jacket folded upon his arm. Anyone watching him would think he was the elite, and they would be right. Once in the plaza, he bought a pack of Clorets from a woman sitting on the ground with drugstore trinkets laid out in front of her. Emptying the packet of two into his mouth, he chewed ungraciously. He didn't particularly care if his cousin knew he had been drinking, but what about the other man? Best to try to be discreet. He gave the woman back the empty Clorets packet and resumed his crisp walk across the broad plaza.

When he reached the Palacio Nacional on the west side of the Zócalo, his boozy mind couldn't think which door to enter through; the building went on forever and the idea of trying to find the correct entrance, exhausting. Stumped, he spat the gum out of his mouth and lit another cigarette. He stood, slightly swaying, to watch a flock of beige doves pick at the black-gray cement. He wondered what could be edible there. Tilting his head to peer more closely, he found respite in the poetry of the soft-colored creatures bobbing at the dark, moody ground, juxtaposed with the radiant yellow sun. When a hand grasped his shoulder, he jumped back and raised his fists, ready to strike.

"For fuck's sake, Liam!" a man said. He had an attaché gripped in both hands, which he held up in defense.

Liam unclenched his fingers and lowered his hands. "Hello, cousin." They shook, then hugged.

Releasing each other, the cousin took a step back, flat-footed and soft; he had a discerning expression. "Are you always this jumpy?"

"I need a toilet."

"You're drunk." The cousin was shorter and dumpier with dark, full hair, whereas Liam's was light and thin. He had a bulbous nose and a blubbery mouth, where Liam's facial features were angled, his mouth almost lipless. They were around the same age and appeared comfortable in each other's presence, except the cousin was perturbed at Liam's drunken indecency, whereas Liam wasn't upset about it at all. They also both spoke Spanish with a Chilean accent: thick, fast, and skidding over their *S*'s and *D*'s.

"You look older," the cousin said.

"So do you." Liam flicked his cigarette toward the birds and watched them fly away.

"We don't have time for coffee. Try to walk straight. And do you have a tie?" His expression puffed and scrunched, he grumbled, "Your father warned me about this."

"Oh, do tell." Liam took a navy-blue paisley tie out of his jacket pocket and put it on. It was crooked, so his cousin readjusted it for him and shook his head in disgust. He then took a resigned deep breath as they walked toward the government building. "This is a very important meeting. How dare you!"

"You sound like my wife."

They went through the correct door and up to the second floor: a cavernous interior with high vaulted ceilings and marble walls and floor. Their steps echoed as they walked. Liam, spotting the men's room, entered, and his cousin waited outside the door for him. When he came back out, he had water splatters on the front of his trousers. His cousin balked and cursed at him, but there was nothing they could do about it. They walked a few more feet down the hall to an office with a placard reading *Chilean Consulate* on the door; they entered without knocking. Liam let out a whistle and waved an index finger at his cousin. "You sly dog. Good buddies with the consulate, eh?" The cousin ignored Liam but took his arm to guide him into the office, along with shutting the door behind them.

A man with a fat chin, flabby sunken cheeks, droopy eyes with lower red rims, and a pencil mustache stood up from behind an elaborately carved Brazilian rosewood desk. His sweaty lips smiled, then fell when he caught sight of the water blotches on Liam's pants. But as good manners dictated, he ignored the disgrace and held out sausage-shaped fingers to shake Liam's hand. "We've been waiting for your arrival. Your cousin has spoken well of you."

Liam made a face as the man's pillowy palm mushed like an overripe banana in his grip. Yet he did force a flurry of etiquette flagellations that important meetings and introductions required while at the same time eyeing the periphery for booze. His eyes snagged sight of the liquor cache. He smiled and went to make his way over to it, but his cousin grabbed his arm and forced him into a seat. Irritated, he sat and eyeballed the man in front of him. He was some sort of uncle, apparently related to another uncle, neither of whom Liam had ever met. Therefore, he wondered if they were truly related and questioned the purpose of meeting with him.

"Senior Gustav has provided the intel we need to find Heraldo and the aunt," the cousin said. "He's also helping fund the investigation."

"How much is your cut?" Liam's jaw wagged, then shut tight.

The man's eyes darted at the cousin. "What?"

The cousin shook his head as though to say "ignore Liam," then leaned into his cousin and whispered, "Shut up." This made Liam want to laugh. He wanted to laugh really, really loudly but didn't. Instead, he sat quietly looking at the sad-faced man in front of him, which made him want to laugh even more. To prevent himself from laughing or talking, he leaned back, stared at the ceiling, which had birds painted on it, and sang "Bluuee birds...." His cousin put a hand on his shoulder. Miffed by the gesture, Liam flicked the hand away with his index finger and was about to leave because he couldn't remember why he was sitting at a desk with mean people. But then the ugly man suggested a drink.

"Liam's tired from his flight. Coffee may be better," the cousin said. "I believe I told you his work back home is filled with demanding responsibilities. Very difficult at times. National Investigative division in Johannesburg, with all the theatrics and impositions a job like that calls for."

The man nodded. Liam queried his mind for something to add, but all he could think was that he had been put on a permanent leave of absence due to a lack of interest in his job or, in other words, a drinking problem. Neither man needed to know that, but he couldn't wipe the smirk off his face. *To think these idiots think I'm important.*

"Is there something funny?" the man asked.

"No, nothing. Not at all." Liam clapped his hands together and got up, brushing his cousin's protests away. He went over to the various bottles of tequila and lifted the bottle of Clase Azul into the air and sucked his teeth with approval. He then turned to the others and said, "Didn't someone say we should have a drink?" then poured three crystal tumblers half full. He put them on a little silver tray and served the two men, then sat back down, pleased with himself, and emptied his drink with a large, noisy gulp. Slamming his empty glass on the desk with a sigh, he reached into his jacket pocket for cigarettes and offered first his cousin, then the fat man, a smoke. They accepted and he lit everyone's, then got up again to bring the bottle of tequila to the party. The two men watched him sit back down with his cigarette tucked into the corner of his mouth and pour the liquor to top off his glass. "Now that's how it's done," Liam said and raised his overly full glass spilling dribbles onto his fingers. "A toast to money." He then downed the entire contents. When he went to pour himself another, his cousin grabbed his arm. "Liam, please, we have things to discuss." His cousin's expression was tight and worried.

Liam stared for a minute at him, then seemed to gain some sort of clarity about the meeting. "Yes...yes, the Unias. Sorry, you see. I'd like to just get going on the job. Now, if I bring him in, Heraldo that is, or is he going by an alias?"

"He hasn't used his real name, Heraldo, for years. Last time he was seen, he was using the name Harry. Yet we think he is currently going by a different alias now."

"Right, but putting the name details aside, what will my cut be? And does it matter if he is alive or not?" Liam's last two words fell sloppy and whiny. "Funny, I used to think taking was so much easier than earning, but now that I have to earn my takings, I need to be paid well. Cuz, you said something about five million. I gather that's for me." Then his mind wandered away somewhere, only to return with gumption. "Well, I'm done. If it's five million or more for me... Let's sign some sort of an agreement, and hell, let me go get him." He got up but instead of going out the door, he went over to the window with the bottle of tequila in his hands and stared out, drinking from the bottle. The men made uneasy grunting noises while they watched him.

"Liam, could you come join us, please?" his cousin said and then began to talk to the man behind the desk while keeping an eye on his wayward relative.

Liam sat back down. "Well, I'm waiting."

"We don't know how much money there is exactly," his cousin sputtered while he tried to snatch the bottle away from Liam. But Liam kept it tucked tightly under his arm.

"What do you mean, you don't know?" Liam queried while slapping at his cousin's petty grabs, convincing him to give up. The cousin then placed a folder in front of Liam, which Liam opened. There was an airplane ticket to Tegucigalpa, Honduras, several thousands of dollars in American Express checks, and a few pages of notes. There were also three photos: a man, a woman, and a boy. Liam, puzzled, asked, "Who are they?"

The man behind the desk shifted in his seat. "What is going on here?" Then, turning to the cousin, he repeated, "What is this?"

Liam shut the folder and sucked on his cigarette. He imagined the tip to be a tit and giggled. His cousin stood up and tugged him out of his chair. "Please excuse us for a moment."

Once outside the room, the cousin shut the door. In a strained voice, he spoke, inches from Liam's face. "If you don't behave, the family won't let you come back to Chile."

"But I don't want to come back," Liam said, wishing he had brought the bottle of tequila with him.

"You'll be cut off. They'll pull strings and you'll lose your job."

Liam smiled because there was no job; didn't his cousin know that? His family also refused to give him any more money unless he helped them out with this matter. He had been a good detective back in Johannesburg. His parents were aware of his clever skills, but his playboy, alcoholic behaviors had them refusing his calls for months, his plea for money ignored. Aware of the divorce and their son's destitute state, his parents decided to give him a family job: find the crooks that stole half their money ten years ago because once again, they, too, were suffering a money loss. The recent devaluation of the Chilean peso had caused them to sell their summer house in the south and two of their yachts. Of course, he said yes, but now he wasn't sure he could do it. Liam slumped onto the cold, tiled hallway floor. "I'm not well, cuz. I have no anchor. I just let go one day. My wife left me. Did you know that?" Not waiting for an answer, he babbled, "My psychiatrist believes my depression and feelings of failure are due to my parents micromanaging my life. I've never been allowed to grow up, and now I don't want to. Too late." He then sat perfectly still staring at the wall in front of him.

"Why wasn't I told this before?" His cousin looked irritated. "It's time to sober up. To stop all this self-pitying nonsense."

"I want to do the job. But I'm a mess. Will you help me?"

"This is very troubling." The cousin paused, then threw his hands in the air. "I'm coming with you."

"Oh, good." Liam smiled and tried to hug his cousin, but he nudged him away. Pouting, he continued, "You do know Heraldo will recognize me. We were good friends as children."

"It's been too long. The last time Heraldo saw you, you were ten."

Liam let out a voluminous belch. The air filled with the nasty effluvium of booze and last night's dinner. He waved his hand in front of his nose. "Chicken molé. She was delightful."

"Damn it! This is the last of your drinking! Cold turkey once we get on the road." His cousin's upper teeth were biting his lower lip. It made Liam smile because he looked like a chipmunk.

"You're sounding like my wife again. You even look a little like her." Then Liam shrugged. "I will not take another drop after today," he said with sincerity. "Now, what about my brother Dori? Will he be joining us? Mummy and Daddy said something about the chore being a family group thing. Although I should get the lion's share of the payout—"

"—I believe they just meant me," the cousin interjected with exasperation. "Dori's gone sailing around Belize with some female and, well, the family have people looking for him. When they find him, he'll be told to help you."

"I thought my younger brother was perfect. Good to know he's not." The cigarette in his hand was burnt to a nub and sizzled at Liam's thumb. He tossed it and lit another. "Is that pencil dick in there really one of us?"

"Yes, and he's my father's brother. He spotted Heraldo at the orphanage in Guatemala. Dori was there too and confirmed his identity. Your parents had given him a picture of Heraldo and the aunt just in case he bumped into him while traveling. Too young to have ever known him." The cousin stopped talking to run his eyes over the deplorable state of Liam and to possibly reflect upon the misfortune of Dori being unable to be found, and now Liam to be the family's savior. He wiped his brow, sighed, and added, "We almost had him and the aunt, but someone tipped them off."

Liam's eyes glistened with amusement. "You know, I never thought they stole the money. I thought Daddy had made it all up because he was in love with the wife...Julieta. You know, Heraldo's mother. But then he killed her, which is odd. Anyway, I don't really care. Morality is stupid." Then he smiled. "When I get my cut, I'm hiding it from my wife." This whimsical happiness faded into a frown. "My name? The family name he knows."

"Use Titlemen. Liam Titlemen. Grammy's name. He shouldn't know it. I'm using a different name too."

The cousin helped Liam off the floor, and they went back into the room and sat down. The man behind the desk was picking at his fingers. The scowl on his face was like a bull struck with banderillas.

"All set," the cousin said.

The man smiled but remained unattractive. He stood up with his glass in hand and raised it. "Let's toast to success and then get on with our day." Liam liked the idea of drinking but found the man extra disgusting. He leaned in toward him and said, "Looking forward to your share, fatso?" His cousin quickly yanked him back. "Please don't mind him. Tomorrow will be a different day for everyone."

After more etiquette "asinine puffery," which Liam mumbled under his breath, the meeting was finally over. His cousin ushered him out of the room and placed Liam's folder filled with directives, money, and pictures into his attaché. "Go sleep this one off. I'll pick you up at four o'clock. Our flight leaves at six."

Chapter
2

The Island

The fitted sheet had come undone, and Lucy's face lay smooshed against the stained mattress. The idea that she was inhaling other people's sex and drool into her lungs and mouth, distasteful. But the type of tired she felt made it impossible to lift her head. It was a beaten-up feeling that had nothing to do with staying up late or abusing alcohol or any other erroneous acts. It was the heat. The heat was like a giant thirsty leech that left a person spun out and gimpy. She wasn't sure if she liked it or hated it, because as much as it was insufferable and entrapping with its lazy, do-nothing grip, it relaxed her. Not a fan of the crunch of life—that is the part of living that made great demands on time and energy—she reveled in the morning's idleness. She luxuriated in the spatial depth of the dream world meeting reality without the compulsion to get up. Her head turned toward the window and its ocean view, she reflected upon the sunless early dawn sea, the hazy air, and the light gray-blue water.

Disrupting her tranquility was a fly that sucked on a lumpy black stain by her left nostril, its bulbous eyes pulsating with every draw. The image gave Lucy the strength to flip her head back onto the pillow. The ceiling, wood painted white, pinned her thoughts with an overwhelming need to sleep again. She let herself slip away, only to awaken seconds later. The fly, now on her thigh, tickled her. She swiped it with the tousled edge of the fitted sheet, and it flew, then landed only inches away. The bug's beady eyes looked at her as though gauging its next move. Once again, she dozed, only to awaken seconds later. She had dreamed the fly was on her nose, and it was. She flicked it off, and the pesty bug disappeared.

Taking in another deep breath of the watery air—the humidity a constant, it occurred to her that it tasted like sand and salt mixed with ocean. *The breakfast bread at the No Name restaurant has the same flavor. Morning air*, she surmised. When the ceiling began to hint of deep pinks as the sun peeked over the horizon, she sighed. "The best part of the day. Not too hot yet that one's insides bake." Then, letting loose an odd snort, she thought, *I'll do nothing today* and laughed because she said the same thing every morning.

Lucy had been staying at the Beach Lodge for two weeks. Every morning she awoke early and analyzed her room as though seeing it for the first time. Angles and shadowed lines at first blurred by the gray alluded to a sense of peace—an amity between motion and stillness of wood. She wondered if it were truly possible to do nothing and let her mind sift through her daily tasks: breathing was something, and eating, along with swimming, lying on the sand, talking to people, and drinking beer. Even sleeping was something. So, the answer was no. But even though it was difficult to completely do nothing, she thought she could become better at it—like some of the locals who sat under a palm tree all day, never moving. But then it occurred to her that the only time a person truly does nothing is when they are dead. What a shame.

Treading her gaze over to the corners of the room, she paused at a thick lacy cobweb with dead bugs. The messy clump of hollow carcasses caused her to think of the fly. Glancing at the lumpy stain again by her head, she saw the fly had returned to drink some more. "So, I didn't kill you. It isn't your time to do nothing."

The stain had the appearance of hardened blood, as though someone had cut themselves, or was it crusty snot? "Where are your friends to help you clean? Or has the spider eaten them all?" Her voice sounded like gravel being scuffed. The fly had a bumbled hairy back laced with green and black stripes. Eyes static, it ignored her.

"Oh, don't be like that. You can be my friend. But just so you know, one day I will have to leave this hotter-than-Hades island. But not while it's hot. And seeing how it's summer, you have nothing to worry about. But a chilly day will come around, and when a chilly day arrives, I will pack my bags and leave. I need the cold for strength."

Her back, pressed against the mattress, had overheated and puddled with sweat. "Fly," she whispered. "I'm hot. Please pick me up and take me to the ocean." The fly tilted its head and flew over to the open window, landing on the screen. "Eh, you forgot me," Lucy barked. The empty bird's nest above the window drew her attention away. It was stuffed between the rafters and the wall. She looked back at the fly, which was nothing but a tiny black speck. She imagined the birds had been locked out, the antithetical situation of the fly being locked in, and the birds being locked out, ironic and deplorable. Then suddenly, overwhelmed and tired from thinking, when a warm breeze fluttered the thin pale curtain, she fell back to sleep once more.

A half-hour later, Lucy awoke again. The high-pitched twittering of several grackles that sat in a palm tree just outside her window was pleasant to listen to. The positioning of the sun, which she could see, was low over the ocean, yellow and glowing. Still early, she thought, yet late enough to get up. "But what day is it?" she mumbled, confused about whether it was Monday or any other day before Sunday. Because if it were Tuesday, the No Name restaurant would be serving bacon at breakfast. "I love bacon," she said aloud. She cleared her throat again of its bullfrog sound and puffed her cheeks to blow out air, then counted, "One, two, three..." And threw herself onto the wooden painted floor. The propulsion caused the half-filled water bottle by her bed to tip over. The spilled water quickly disappeared through the cracks.

"What...shit...not again," a male voice shouted from below, followed by, "Lucy! What the hell!"

Crawling onto her hands and knees, Lucy laughed. "Poor Freddy."

She then stood and smelled her armpits, cringed, stripped, put her bathing suit on (all within minutes), and stomped on the floor with her foot. When there was no response from below, she knelt, placing her mouth by a small opening, and shouted, "Freddy, put your suit on. Time to swim! Then breakfast!"

Still no response.

"Freddy, I think it's bacon Tuesday!"

Still no response.

Sitting back, she pouted, *it would be better to swim without him.* It would be calmer to be alone in the sea because Freddy talked a lot. Not that she didn't like talking to him, but he made it hard to hear the waves and birds.

She opened her door, stepped out into the hallway, locked the bolt, then bounded down the steps and out the back door to the beach. There had been a party with tiki torches, booze, and barbecued meats the night before. Several elderly locals were walking around with garbage bags, picking up paper plates, bottles, plastic forks, and knives.

Lucy had gone to the party with Freddy and the Italians: a blond girl and two scrubby-looking olive-skinned boys in their late teens. The small group was traveling around Central America for a few months before starting at the University of Milan in the fall. They had come to the island to learn how to scuba dive, and if all went well, to obtain a certificate.

Since meeting the threesome, Lucy decided speaking Spanish with an Italian accent was posher than any other accent; therefore, she made a point to talk to the blond girl and the boys as much as possible to perfect it. At the party, they chatted about Bolognese sauce and rice versus wheat. The Italians had been drinking rum straight out of a bottle, and it wasn't long before Freddy and Lucy lost them in the crowd. Left to talk to each other, Lucy and Freddy sipped tepid beer while standing on the periphery of the party watching people dance. The band, a colorfully dressed group with five steel drummers, two saxophones, three ukulele players, and four singers, played Caribbean jazz tunes. Lucy often danced at these parties, but tonight she was content just watching.

"Looking in from the outside," Freddy had called what they were doing.

"Observing our environment...getting to know it," Lucy had remarked.

"Can't."

"Can't what?" Lucy asked while watching a man and a woman gyrate their hips to the music.

"Ever know it."

"Why is that?"

"It's not your world."

"It could be if I stayed here long enough," Lucy shouted. Every instrument in the ten-piece band had begun playing a crashing crescendo.

"Maybe?" Freddy shouted back.

"What?"

"If you lived here permanently, you'd just hang with the expats," Freddy said into her ear. The crowd had gone wild over the exploding tune.

"I already have local friends. Ernesto."

"Ernesto, the Beach Lodge owner? Foreigner. Honduran parents but born in Chelsea, *Maaassachusetts.* That is how you pronounce that state?"

"Close enough... Okay, Juanita and Fabio," Lucy countered.

"Juanita's ten. And Fabio's a bird. Poached, no doubt."

"Mosquito Coast bird, still Honduran," she retorted. Freddy responded with an exasperated stare that made Lucy laugh. "Am I torturing you, Freddy?"

Chuckling, he kicked sand over her feet. "Possibly."

Now the next morning, Lucy desired to swim, to wipe away the nighttime heat and fanfare, along with the morning grime. The ocean was barely moving, just a soft push onto the beach, the color blue, diaphanous, seeming drinkable until a plastic bag and a half-eaten chicken leg floated into view. She looked back toward the people stuffing garbage into bags. They were bent over, thin, and wrinkled like dried seaweed. She wondered if that was a rule here—that is, the young partied and the old cleaned up. She wanted to tell them to clean the ocean too, but maybe that was too bratty. Breathing in deep, as though trying to center the contrasting mess with the bright sun and the sparkling ocean, she realized that once again she was looking in from the outside and wished Freddy was with her so they could discuss the matter further.

"Lucy!" She turned her head toward the Beach Lodge. It was Freddy.

"Since you woke me up, you owe me breakfast." He was galumphing over the sand, arms swinging, hair wild and bouncing freely. A hefty, meaty fellow, solid but not fat, he looked like an upright red-headed walrus goofing its way to the water's edge.

"I won the bet yesterday. Remember, I bet that the parrot would say my name," Lucy shouted while letting her feet dip into the ocean. Once he reached her, he abruptly stopped, bent over, and put his hands on his knees, huffing and puffing.

"You're wheezing?" Lucy poked him, teasingly.

"Lack of sleep. The heat's miserable." He stood up straight and smiled. "Hell, it's already horribly hot." Beads of sweat prickled his upper lip and puddled under his translucent blue eyes. Then, looking suspect at Lucy, he said, "I don't think that bet, yesterday, was fair at all."

"How can it not be fair?"

"You consider the bird your friend. I think you two are in cahoots with each other."

Lucy laughed. "You're daffier than I am."

Freddy glanced away at the ocean. "Is that a chicken leg?" He then coughed, made a hideous sound, and spat a loogie onto the ground. "Okay, breakfast is on me."

Lucy smiled while kicking sand over the spit. "Do you ever wonder why Lyla left you?"

"Don't be so prudish. Lyla likes my spit. In fact, she loves it. She had to go back home... That was all. You know, school."

"Do you think you'll visit her?"

"I miss her. But my home is in Denmark, and she lives in Australia. We made plans to meet in Thailand for Christmas break—that's if I ever leave here."

"First cool day, I'm out," Lucy said, pulling Freddy's T-shirt to walk on. "Let's swim before eating but not near the plastic baggie and the chicken. Down the beach, away from where the party was."

"You keep saying that, but you don't." His tone was accusing; he was also slightly backpedaled against her grip.

"Don't what?"

"Leave."

"So do you," Lucy said, stopping to glance at Freddy.

Freddy scowled. "I'm not ready to leave because I don't want to do anything serious, whereas you are always pretending like you're ready when you're not." He then pulled his shirt out of Lucy's hand and asked. "What about the careers you talk about? And your Spanish? I thought you wanted to become fluent. Possibly better without an Italian accent."

"Why would I want to change my accent?" Lucy said, perplexed.

A pelican flew over them, creating a shadow; they both looked up. Standing still, they watched it land where the party had been and waddled around, poking at the random half-filled garbage bags. Freddy's mouth puckered into an O. It was as though he wanted to say something but couldn't think of what.

Having walked several yards down the beach, they both appraised the waters in front of them. It was perfect. Calm with a mesmerizing shimmer and not a speck of anything not worthy of an ocean's glory. Their silence, unusual for them, held them steadfast. Then Freddy sighed, placed his hands on his hips, and declared, "I love living here," his voice soft and ethereal. Turning toward Lucy, he smacked his lips. "The hotel is only ten kroner a night. I spend around twenty-three a day on food and beer. That's a total of thirty-three kroner a day. I like doing nothing. I like spending hardly anything." He then puffed his chest out as though proud of himself and waited for a response.

"What's that in dollars?"

"I think five."

"Five dollars is something. And breathing is something too." Lucy chuckled, thinking about her earlier conversation with herself. "Besides, no one alive can do nothing. One can only do nothing if one is dead."

Freddy laughed. "Aren't we being philosophical this morning?"

"I guess—" she said, sighing. "Well, I'm working on doing as little as possible. But not nothing." Pausing, she grinned with a glint of mischievousness in her eyes. "Like some of the locals. I'd like to sit under a tree all day and not move."

Freddy laughed briefly as his attention wandered off to watch an old man with a pitchfork walk by them. Refocusing, he said, "Come to think of it, we shouldn't use the word *nothing* because, if we want to be philosophical about it, what it really is, is just not being serious. Like me, I have no desire to be serious about anything."

"And, you know, it's not being frivolous."

"Nor trivial."

"No, it, well...just doing whatever we feel like," Lucy said, looking at Freddy, who had gone back to watching the old man walk over to a trash pile and lunge his pitchfork into the middle of it. He then tossed the heap into a wheelbarrow that an old lady had brought over.

"On second thought, I take doing what I want to do very seriously. Unlike you, I am serious about doing what I want." Lucy spoke, now, too, watching the elderly man and woman.

"What?" Freddy gasped.

"But one day, although I only spend...let me think, I think I spend less than you, even though my room has a better view. I spend four-fifty a day. That is around sixteen hundred and something a year." Lucy looked down at her toes. "I don't have that much money. I have less than a year to be carefree." Lightly biting her lower lip, she sucked at her teeth and looked back over at the cleanup crew. "Until then, I plan to be as seriously carefree as I can." Pausing to breathe, she added, "Those people over there, they don't get paid. It's all volunteer. So, I'm going to say they are doing what they want to."

"Not sure. It's like if you had kids. And your kids don't pick up after themselves, so you have to do it or step on their mess and trip."

Lucy squinted. "I think you're right."

Freddy broke out in a hearty guffaw. "Let's call ourselves the 'happy-go-luckies.' Since most people would think just eating, breathing, swimming, drinking, and—"

"—playing."

"Are do-nothing stuff, but we will set them straight if they ask."

"Taking time to smell the roses." Lucy smiled.

"Studying the art of tranquility." Freddy beamed.

Watching the tiny waves push onto the sand, they threw their towels into a heap on the beach and walked into the water. Freddy ran first. When he reached where the ocean met his thighs, he dove. Lucy followed, she, too, diving in headfirst. Together, they swam, making big kicking splashes, which echoed like pebbles skidding across glass. "Wake up, sea, sky, and earth. We're the happy-go-luckies!" Lucy shouted.

Settling in, Freddy lay on his back and sang a song in Danish, while Lucy paddled into the shallows, chasing little fish. She then stopped and stood up. "I want life to stay like this forever."

Freddy looked at her. "Impossible."

Chapter
3

The Call

Josey Wales stood at the back door of the No Name restaurant with a bucket of fish that he had caught that morning. It was eight o'clock, and he had already been up for three hours. Unable to sleep due to a recurring bad dream, he had gotten up, made coffee, and sat on his own porch looking at the dark ocean and the distant lights of fishing boats on the horizon. Halfway through his second cup of coffee, he went over to the dive shop and grabbed his fishing pole. Standing at the end of his dock, he managed to pull in two medium-sized groupers and a snapper fit for a king. Not having a freezer, he often sold his excess catches to either the No Name or the Porch Bar and Grill. This morning he wanted a loaf of pan de coco, a No Name specialty.

The dream had been about the family's escape, a year ago, from El Puente. It always started off in the same realistic manner. Having completed the selling of a large building in the next town over, El Pueblito, he finds himself sitting on his bed at the orphanage where he had been living. He is counting money. Eleanor, his lover and roommate, walks in. Her dark, thick hair is loose around an oval ghostly white face. Her green eyes appear to be larger and ignited by something important. She has mud on her legs and arms; her clothing is torn. In real life, this scene somewhat happened. It was just not as fluid and warped the way the dream juxtaposed images into slow-moving objects and thoughts. In real life, she had gone over to her bed because she was having an anaphylactic reaction to fire ant bites. But in the dream, she walks over to him and starts telling him to run. He ignores her and keeps counting the money, even though he desperately wants to get a cloth and wipe the mud off her. But he feels the money is more important. She begins yelling, "Run!" He pretends she isn't there, and she disappears. He is glad she is gone because "why was she yelling?" He stuffs the money into his bag and stands up. Now relaxed, he misses her. He wants to hold her, smell the nape of her neck. When he looks around the room, it's empty. Even his bed has disappeared. He feels sad and lonely. He opens the door and calls for her. But when he steps out of the room, he finds himself standing on the bank of a river. The waters, tumultuous, grab his feet, and he is swept into the torrent current. He begins to swim. His bag in his hand, he drags it along. When he stops to look up, two men are standing above him. The noses of their guns in his face. He wakes up. Without fail, every time, he awakens drenched in sweat and gripped with anxiety. Because there is never any point to go back to sleep, he makes himself a cup of coffee and sometimes a stiff alcoholic drink. The dream, disquieting, always caused an unbearable restlessness.

The cook at the No Name opened the back door and waved Josey in. He placed the bucket of fish on the floor, whereupon the cook whistled at the size of the catch. The cook, a short, hairy man, gave Josey a loaf of pan de coco and several lempiras for the fish, then poured them both a cup of coffee. They sat down on wooden stools in the rustic stone kitchen and began to chat about whether the summer storms will cause damage to the island this year, then commented on the new batch of tourists who had recently come in from the mainland. Most of their tone was nonjudgmental and even less committal, but they both agreed the new tourists were bad tippers. When Josey's assistant, Mateo, appeared in the kitchen out of breath, the two men perked up. "Boss, yah have a message to call home, ASAP." Mateo's words sent a frozen chill coursing through Josey's veins. He placed his half-full cup of coffee in the sink and hurried out. The radio was to be used for emergency purposes only. It was either his aunt or, if something had happened to his aunt, Oggie, his nephew.

The rear of the restaurant was built on boulders that protruded out into the ocean. Josey walked up over them to take a shortcut to the Porch Bar and Grill. The Australians, along with another business owner named Milly, owned the only two means of contacting the mainland, a transistor radio. While up on the rocks, he heard his name being called. He turned and looked at the beach. It was Lucy with a fellow he perceived to be her boyfriend but wasn't sure since he had been with another last week.

"Josey!" Lucy shouted while waving to him. "Eat breakfast with us?"

"Another time!" He yelled back and jumped off the rocks down to the path below.

It was hot in the little back room of the Porch Bar and Grill. Sweat beaded Josey's chest, face, and back, not a speck of wind in the closed quarters to cool him off, as he clicked the receiver and twisted the nobs to contact the correct frequency. "Auntie, what's happening?"

"They know where you are. It seems that Alex fellow from the orphanage was drunk in a bar in Copan." His aunt's thick Mapuche accent and broken Spanish faded out and in through the frequency static. But Josey, used to it, could decipher enough. "Alex said he saw you in Roatan. Wasn't it months ago that you were there?" She continued. "Or have you gone back over since? Anyway, it's only a matter of time before they figure out, they have the wrong island. Mi dios, this chase has lasted a long time. It started over a decade ago. It's 1992...where has all the time gone?" His aunt was babbling. It was something she had begun doing since turning seventy. It seemed the stress of trying to keep their small family safe from his father's former business partner had begun to take its toll. But then it was beating up Josey too. He was tired of it...very tired of it.

"You'd think they would give up by now," the aunt continued. "He loved your mother."

"Strange to kill the person you love," Josey stated, words he had repeated over and over again throughout the years.

"Their greed will never end well for them." Her voice trailed off, the words she spoke, like a memorized script.

"Who told you the news?"

"*Hijo.*" Although she was his aunt, she called him *son*. "When you get here, we will discuss it. Your passport. You need to do something about the dates."

"I know...I'll leave this morning."

"Let's go to Australia." She then chuckled. "God loves us. He will never forsake us."

Silence.

In Josey's youth, he had been devout. The test of strength. The imposed sacrifice for Jesus' sufferings. But as time went on, he saw that the poetry of Jesus had been twisted and wronged, and used to do more bad than good. Yet, he couldn't help but think the only reason they were still alive was due to "divine intervention." Acknowledging they needed all the help they could get, he concurred. "Yes, Auntie, the heavens have had our backs. Let's hope they still do."

"Hijo, you would be bored if life were easy. God made you a strong man and has fated you to succeed." She often said these words. He knew she felt guilty for asking him to leave England to help her. They would have found him eventually, but no matter how many times he told her this, she still apologized. His aunt had loved the idea that he was studying at Oxford, a life he hardly remembered anymore, and when he did, the memories seemed like he had read them in a book about someone else. The bars, the girls, the array of restaurants, and his dorm room to his flat on the Thames, a sophisticated life he had loved. But when it stopped, suddenly, just like today—a phone call from his aunt, pitting him between ignoring danger or taking the precautionary route of running, he ran. Underneath the façade of a rich, playboy life lay the foundation of a very simple man. He missed the sound of a rooster crowing in the morning and the smell of tortillas cooking on a fire. When he had first moved into the orphanage as a teacher to help his aunt sell land in Guatemala, it was an adjustment but a good one. He had found love and almost married a woman named Jacquelina. When it failed because neither he nor she was ready, they both found warmth and comfort in the arms of another. She Cadmael, and he, Eleanor. *Eleanor, my card playing, rum swizzling, Eleanor.* But no man can be with another when on the run.

"Hijo, are you there?" His aunt woke him from his thoughts.

"Yes," he said, realizing he had drifted off.

"Jacquelina got married," she said.

He laughed. "How do you find out so much?"

"I still know people in the village."

He was happy for his ex-fiancée. He was over her. He had been over her for a long time. It was Eleanor that still haunted him.

"I'm cooking carne asada for lunch. See you soon, *mi amor.*" She clicked off.

Josey put the radio piece back in its holder. Taking a deep breath, he brushed his short dyed-blond hair back and stared out the small, closed window. Aurora and Dan, the Australians who owned the place, were by a patch of purple flowers discussing something. Although Josey slept with the occasional good-looking vacationing diver, he was always happy to see them leave. Tired of the diaspora and one-night flings, he grumbled, "I want to grow old and stand with a significant other by a patch of flowers to discuss the morning, evening, and day." Overall, he wasn't too sure what he wanted, except that he missed being in love.

He stayed in the sweltering heat of the room with sweat and the pulse of his heart keeping him company; it was similar to the way a cut, or a broken arm, masked psychological misery. Allowing memories of the orphanage to bombard his thoughts, the face of Eleanor crept in. "I see you in my dream, but you disappear," he whispered. Besides, he had heard she was with another. Shrugging, he got up, tossed a couple of lempiras down on the counter, and walked out into the yard to thank the Australians for the use of their radio. He knew he must get going. If his family had to flee again, he needed to get his paperwork in order and the only place to do that was Tegucigalpa.

Chapter
4

The No Name

The No Name restaurant was one of those places with a name that lacked any signs to indicate what it might be. Even the owner, Lilly, was nebulous about what to call her restaurant. She called it various odd phrases such as *No saber ni papa de una tomate*—not knowing a potato from a tomato, *Ponerse Las Pilas*—slang for 'wake up,' and *Creernos la última Coca-Cola del travelers*—we think we're better than everyone else. But since the locals went with No Name because it was easier to remember, Lilly often did too.

It was a cement building with low ceilings. When entering, one had to walk down stony steps and duck to get in through the small doorway. The floor tiles were all mismatched: some gray, others white, and a few pinks and purples. To the left side of the restaurant, half the wall was missing, which allowed diners to watch the ocean while eating. The force of the waves that crashed on the rocks outside gave the place a constant breeze and a cool, misting spray. Through a door to the back, a cigar-making business took place, and upstairs was the owner's residence. Lucy, Freddy, other foreigners, and locals went to the No Name because it was cheap, and the chef, the hairy older brother of the owner, mixed cheese into the scrambled eggs. And of course, there was Bacon Tuesday. But besides all of that—it was the only breakfast joint in town.

To Lucy's and Freddy's chagrin, it turned out to be Sunday, which made them wonder where the week had gone. Trying to recount what had transpired over the past couple of days, they did realize that the Italians had arrived during the week, along with several other foreigners who wanted to learn how to scuba dive, which was normal. Most people who came to the island were there for the diving.

"When did they all arrive?" Lucy puzzled.

"Can't remember. To think, all divers and no happy-go-luckies," Freddy said.

"I guess we're unique."

"I like that."

Lucy stopped talking to look around the restaurant for the driest area. She glanced back at Freddy and smiled, her mind having wandered back to a former discussion, "Okay, I confess. It's not just the heat that keeps me from leaving. I don't want to leave, but I'm torn—you know, pulled to do something like get a job. But now that I am happy-go-lucky, I'm not going to say I want to leave anymore because that is definitely something. Hell, Freddy. We have titles now. Like royalty."

Freddy laughed. "Why not? King Freddy Happy-Go-Lucky."

Then unexpectedly, she buzzed, "Oh, I have another local friend."

Freddy jerked his head around and stared at her, then put his hands on his hips and waited.

"Josey Wales."

"The dive instructor? He's not a native either. Canadian or is he British? I'm not sure but not Honduran," Freddy said, grabbing a clump of one-ply napkins that had been placed on the table. Handing a bunch to Lucy, they began mopping up the puddles on the seats so they could sit. Working away, Freddy asked, "Do you think that is his real name? Josey Wales. It's a Hollywood name. Clint Eastwood movie. Outlaw."

Lucy bit her lower lip. "Haven't seen it. Okay, so I have two true Honduran friends, Juanita and Fabio." Pensive, she put her finger in the air. "But I'm putting Ernesto and Josey as half-locals because they live here. Two halves make a whole. So, I have three local friends."

Freddy ground his teeth together. Appearing miffed, he exhaled and sat without comment. Then, unable to hold back, he said, "That is preposterous."

"Why do you have such a good English-speaking vocabulary?"

"Back home I watch a lot of American movies."

Lucy squinched her nose. "They've never helped my vocabulary."

Once seated, they patiently waited for Lilly to take their order, a stout four-foot-tall woman with three wiry black hairs on her chin. Bulgy-busted, she liked to wear skimpy cocktail dresses, her cleavage often exposed down to her navel. Presently, she was in the tobacco manufacturing room with a weathered *Vogue* magazine inches from her nose. The room was lit by nothing more than a streak of sun that moved from floor to table to wall as the morning wended its way toward noon. The airy cave-like area resembled an ancient ruin with its chipped gray walls and low ceiling. Lucy and Freddy figured it was the business's proximity to the ocean that gave her cigars a flavorful combination of seaweed, fish, and a silty sand taste, a seasoning the bread and the morning air contained too. People on the island liked the flavor, and the cigar-making business was profitable. And because Freddy and Lucy were never in a rush to go anywhere, for two mornings in a row, they had helped roll cigars into thumb-size stogies—a mindless task that did take dexterity. Too loose and the cigars fell apart, too tight and the cigars wouldn't stay lit. The work wasn't for everyone and instilled a sense of pride and accomplishment in those that could do it. Although the feeling of doing wasn't something the two happy-go-luckies sought knowingly.

Lucy, while sitting in her chair, wobbly on the uneven floor, tried to find the best position for it and burst out, "I have one more local friend, Lilly."

Freddy's mouth made an *O* but was not able to form any words to comment.

"*Café, mis chiquitos?*" Lilly was standing by their table with two tin pots with spouts. Without waiting for an answer, she poured the thick, soupy coffee and milk into two glass mugs that were on a nearby tray and placed the beverages in front of them. Lucy's and Freddy's eyes darted toward her cleavage and then abruptly away. Lilly gave a mild shake; the loose skin yo-yoed back and forth, which grabbed their attention again. She then stood up straight and nodded at her brother to make breakfast. Since there wasn't any bacon, because it wasn't bacon Tuesday yet, breakfast would consist of scrambled eggs with cheese, fried coconut bread, and slices of either pineapple or papaya. Today, it was pineapple.

"Let's visit Fabio after breakfast," Lucy suggested, sipping her coffee.

"The bird again. Why?" Freddy said, eyeing her suspiciously.

"I bet I can get him to say your name."

"And?"

Lucy shifted in her seat and scrunched her lips together. "The winner gets tomorrow's breakfast."

"Didn't we do this already today?"

"You owed me breakfast today. The bet was yesterday, and Fabio said my name, not yours."

"You're very suspect. I have a feeling you've already taught him to say Freddy," Freddy remarked while studying Lucy's face as though skeptical about who she was.

"He's never mentioned it," Lucy said. She wanted more coffee and waved her hand at Lilly. When Lilly didn't notice, too busy rolling cigars on the rusty metal table and chatting with her sisters, who had come into the restaurant like a torrent of busybodies with bags full of tobacco leaves and yapping about food, men, and loose girls, Lucy got up and helped herself, saying, "So with no practice, I will get him to say your name." She topped off their coffees and sat back down.

"I don't want to bet. It's ruining my budget." He let his mouth rest on his mug, then took a sip and put the mug down on the table. With a teasing glint in his eyes, he said, "Lyla, Milly, and I saw you when you walked off the ferry the day you arrived. We both said, oh, look, another backpacker. And she's Amer—"

"—American. How could you tell?" Lucy asked, her eyes boring into him. She knew travelers and locals alike made comments about new arrivals. It was a game to try to guess what country the person came from and whether they were cool or a goober. "I think I could pass for Italian," she said, sniffing as though something an Italian would do.

Freddy guffawed. "If you like Italians so much, why aren't you in Italy?"

"I read somewhere that if a person can speak Spanish and English, they can communicate with 80 percent of the people in the world. Doesn't work that way with Italian." Just then, Lilly slapped full plates of food in front of them. Before she stepped away, Lilly jiggled her breasts over the food like salt and pepper shakers. The eggs glistened with buttery cheese, and the pan de coco fried in coconut oil had them eating with fork and fingers. After a few fervent bites, Lucy chewed the next spoonful of eggs with a lazy jaw and continued, "I think I look like I could also be from any European country, like France but not Germany." Lucy put her chin in her hands and let her eyes rest on Freddy.

"What about a Scandinavian country?"

"I hardly have the stature of a Viking."

Freddy spread his arms open and glanced down at his well-formed but hefty body and smiled. "What do you mean by that?" When Lucy didn't respond, Freddy smacked his lips. With an amused glimmer in his eyes, he said, "It's the walk. Americans walk duckish." Then he sat back, as though waiting for a storm.

Not taking the bait, she nonchalantly replied, "You might have something there. I'm going to work on walking differently. What do you think of the blond Italian's walk?"

Freddy opened his mouth to say something but then shut it. He clunked his teeth together and burst out laughing.

After a moment of silence, he grinned. "I'm changing the subject."

"To Fabio saying your name?"

"No. Last night, one of the Italian boys told me about a lost spring at Squash Beach. I think we should go find it."

"Other side of the island," Lucy said, glancing over at Lilly and her sisters. "They must have different mothers or fathers because none of them look alike."

"It will be an adventure. And what fun if we find it."

"I was going to do as little as possible today—sit under a palm tree with some locals and not move," Lucy said, bringing her attention back to Freddy.

"Not that again."

"Mmm...finding a lost spring does sound like fun...maybe. But first Fabio." She then smiled. "A bet."

"Are you trying to swindle me so you can stay non-serious longer?"

"Possibly, but it truly is fifty-fifty whether he says your name or not. We're talking about a bird." Lucy looked directly into Freddy's light blue, almost gray eyes. In the muted light of the restaurant, she noticed he freckled instead of tanning, and although she didn't find him handsome, he was inquisitive and laughed easily. She was glad he had knocked on her door after Lyla left. "I bet Lyla misses you," she said watching him place eggs on his fried bread and take a messy lunge at it.

He wiped his chin, swallowed hard, then muttered, "It would be nice."

It amused Lucy that he was such a messy eater. Looking down at the floor, she saw pebbles of eggs and a couple of beans under his chair. They had been only hanging out together for a few days. The weeks prior, she had spent her time either visiting various acquaintances or alone. There were the long walks on the beach, swimming, and meandering to the store. She liked to walk with Fabio or Juanita and sometimes Arnoldo, their father. Late afternoons, if not reading under a palm tree on the beach, she would sit with Ernesto, a very fat man who drank beer all day while he sat in a small plastic chair by the front door of the Beach Lodge which he owned.

Josey Wales, the dive instructor, she found handsome. She liked to visit him too. He showed her how to fill up the scuba tanks with gas. "Twenty-one percent oxygen, 78 percent nitrogen, and approximately 1 percent other trace gases, usually argon," he explained the mixture. But for the most part, she found him to be a quiet, pensive fellow who liked to stick to teaching, reading, and himself. He never went to the Porch and Bar Grill, the expat bar, to have a beer or dinner, a bar where Lucy went every night to eat. His dive shop was tucked in a cove on the leeward side of the island, which was also away from the town and restaurants. Because it was off the beaten path, it caused her visits to seem premeditated. She didn't want to dive. It was too expensive. But she liked to help Josey with the shop: cleaning, putting gear away, and if there was not a thing to do, she often just sat and told Josey about her day, even though she had already told the others, Fabio, Juanita, etc. Her peripatetic life was amazingly mindless and whimsical. But with Freddy, life had changed. She hadn't seen Josey in two days, except for this morning, and now she had constant companionship. To her surprise, she enjoyed it, even though she slightly missed Josey.

"No, I'm not a swindler, but I do like the game of chance," Lucy finally said, interrupting the quiet.

Hearing a crash, they turned toward the sea and watched a fury of waves barrel onto the rocks. The restaurant pointed north toward the open ocean, which caused occasional mayhem. The spray threw huge sheaths of water everywhere. A table rolled onto its side, and a chair slid across the room. Lucy and Freddy stood up with their plates and mugs in hand and walked outside where two chairs and a small table had been placed by the entrance under a dragon fruit vine. When they sat down, dangling melons brushed their backs.

"I wonder where that is coming from."

"A distant ship? Who knows; the ocean's fickle," Freddy said.

Lucy returned to their earlier conversation: "Back home but not often, I'd go to the casinos and play craps. I'm good at it."

"I don't like gambling. A waste of hard-earned cash."

"It's only breakfast. But we could make it a—" She dug into her fanny pack and pulled out a small, weightless Honduran coin— "*Pilito*. It's not even worth a penny. Sounds reasonable, eh?"

"Gosh, I never know what to do with those things. Yes, a pilito it is."

"Okay, I bet I can get Fabio to say your name." Lucy put her hand out to shake Freddy's. The sun beating down on their faces caused them to squint at each other.

"Does this mean we're going to Squash Beach?" Freddy inquired, shading his eyes.

"Yes."

An air of buoyancy swept over his posture. "Ha-ha—you may

make a gambler out of me. I have a pocket full of pilitos." Now laughing, he stood up and held out his hand, and they shook.

Lucy chuckled—the morning was turning out to be splendid—but then kneaded her brow as the thought of a hike, bothersome. "We need provisions." She added, "Two birds with one stone—Fabio lives at the fruit store. And we can buy water and other stuff, and—"

"—Oh, not nice. Fabio is a bird. Better to use the Danish version. Two flies with one smack," Freddy said and went inside to pay.

Chapter
5

Lucy

Before Lucy arrived on the island, she and two friends from college had been backpacking around Guatemala and Honduras. The girls had just graduated: the pageantry, the parents, the bawling babies, the treading eyes and powdery faces of grandparents, a rabbit grazed by the staging, all a magnified end to a beginning.

When the short-felt pride and excitement were usurped by expectations of adulthood, the flash of a career, marriage, babies, and a yard dizzied Lucy into a free fall of uncertainty because, how quickly one's life is over. To stave off the inevitable, Lucy and her two friends (sisters), an archaeology major and an anthropology major, believed a trip to Central America to see the Mayan ruins sang of future résumé jargon coupled with not having to enlist in what was presumed to be—their parents' lives.

The two sisters had received a small sum of money to help them with their next step in life, while Lucy, earlier in the year, had inherited money due to the passing of a relative. Collectively it wasn't much, but overall, enough. Lucy, an English major, equated ruins with romance and packed her bags with images of Kate chasing Heathcliff through the Yorkshire moors. She also fancied herself to be an up-and-coming bilingual patron of the world. She bought with glee a notebook, pen, and a Spanish-English dictionary, and practiced certain phrases before leaving, ie, '¿dónde esta el baño'—where is the bathroom?' and '¿cuánto cuesta este?'—how much is this?' It was all so doable, even though there are no moors in Honduras.

In Tikal, Guatemala, it rained. The sky melded into stone, and the clouds smothered the tops of the temples like snowy Himalayan peaks. Lucy watched her friends awash in the blurry gray water march up the steps as she stood below, a fuchsia-colored umbrella above her head, the idea of heights horrifying. "Someone has to write the letter home," she had said, tongue in cheek, sipping on pineapple juice at the base.

When in Copan, Honduras, the girls stood shoulder to shoulder gazing at the very tall Nohuch Mul ruin, its height boundless. When evening drew near, Lucy and her friends bought margaritas while in town with a couple of fat, brassy-haired British girls. Two older men joined them. They claimed to be government officials. One of the men was named Liam, and he was from South Africa, a lanky pasty-white drunkard who boasted he was related to the president of Chile. He mentioned the president's name, but Lucy, who despised politics, found the topic boring and complicated in the way an on-going lie stops making sense; she had no need to learn the names of politicians. The other man, Liam's cousin, was a round fellow who seemed uptight and very, very serious about the mission they were on. He constantly complained about the heat and worried about snakes and bugs. Liam, a much more carefree fellow, constantly drank from a brass booze bottle in his coat pocket, slurred his words often, and flooded the girls with compliments. Lucy and the girls liked his fluid

South African accent mixed with Spanish until he fell into a mess of drunken drool. He also kept insisting that they must know of a man named Heraldo or Harry because he was very handsome. He babbled on that the Heraldo-Harry man loved women and was very seductive: "Irresistible to the female persuasions' libido." He flashed them a picture of him. The picture was of a boy in his mid-teens, and the girls wondered why the man thought they would find such a juvenile, 'irresistible.' Liam explained it was his only photo and to imagine him older. "Delicious, uh?" The girls didn't care, nor was he familiar. It was while looking at Heraldo-Harry's picture that a scorpion bit Liam's cousin, sending him to the hospital and Liam with him. Later, through village gossip, they heard the cousin had passed away and that the man named Liam kept mumbling, "My poor dear cousin, but hallelujah! All the more for me."

Lucy and her American friends said goodbye to the British girls. They had been traveling for a year already and needed to return home to England. The three Americans took a chicken bus to La Ceiba to catch a mail boat to the Mosquito Coast, also known as *Gracias de Dios hemos salidas* (Thank God we have exits.) It was where the Tawahka Anthropological Reserve was located and thrilled Lucy's companions to see it.

But plans changed. When the mail-boat assistant, a dark-haired woman with green eyes, lovely looking, young, and strong, stepped off the boat to help them on, the German behind her bolted forth and stopped Lucy and her companions from getting on. He had red dreads tied up like swizzle sticks, and he growled, "Don't go. Lots of fer-de-lance. The bite kills with pain. Lotta pain. But worse, the sand fleas. Yah can't sleep. They're everywhere. I just hope I haven't caught Tungiasis. Disfigurement of limbs."

"Alex, it's beautiful there. Stop ruining possible fun," the dark-haired woman had snapped.

"Eleanor, don't lie," Alex charged back. Then the two began to catapult insults at each other. It ended with the German storming away only to turn back around and shout, "I know where your lover is, but I'll never tell you." He laughed. Then the German named Alex grumbled off toward town as the mail carrier, Eleanor, stared at him with her mouth agape.

The girls giggled at the tiff. They also changed their minds about the coastal jungle and set their sights on Belize and the Altun Ha ruins. They went to board a bus by Swinford Park, but while hanging out with the birds and the trees waiting for the bus, they met a beautiful-looking man named Dorian Titlemen. He told them to call him Dori and that although he was originally from Chile, he now lived in Halifax, Nova Scotia. He was spending a year sailing around Central America to find himself, along with getting out of the cold. He had a pleasant, almost beautiful face, like one of those Roman statues in a museum, only with eyes that moved, and he was bronzed from the sun, and his blue eyes held light and dark and a worldliness none of them had ever known. He had a sailboat. It was a sloop-rigged L. Francis Herreshoff H-28. A twenty-eight-foot boat wasn't large for a seafaring sailboat, but this one was long enough, wide, and sported a shallow draft for comfortable shoreline sailing and sleeping. It was the color of a dark green night and had a white pinstripe outlining the lacquered mahogany railing, which was dappled with shiny brass cleats. There were three off-white sails, and the mast flew the Honduran flag, along with a blue and red Belizean flag because he'd purchased the boat there from a fellow named Dan. Lucy immediately fell in love. But finding herself tongue-tied due to his beauty, when they sailed up the shoreline of Honduras for a couple of sultry, drunken days, her more talkative travel companions ended up below having sex with him, one at a time. Lucy, although heartbroken, was fine with keeping herself chaste. Her boyfriend in college had run off with another, and she felt love, crushes, and sex were all overrated, at least for the time being.

When Dori dropped the girls off in La Ceiba harbor, he mumbled that he needed to find a woman he loved. This statement confused Lucy's friends, but they took it in stride. The girls not only wanted to see archaeological ruins during their trip but to have memories, such as sex with a handsome man on a sailboat, a wonderful tale to tell when they got home.

The woman he was searching for was Eleanor, and she had left him one day when they had argued. Lucy remembered that possibly the woman with the mail boat was Eleanor. She was going to mention this to Dori but stopped herself. She felt Dori was a cad and didn't blame Eleanor, if that was her name, for leaving him.

Back in La Ceiba they decided to visit the post office before leaving for the ruins in Belize. The post office was in a brown, stone building in a dusty area with flat one-story structures. It just so happened that a two-week-old telegram was waiting for the sisters. It was from their mother. The news was about their father's health. It wasn't good, and their mother needed them immediately by her side. With biting tears of anger, confusion, and fear of losing a true loved one, the two sisters got on the next plane for home. They all had been having such a terrific time. Lucy wanted more and had no intention of departing just yet for the States.

But when she did think about a job, she wondered if becoming a psychologist or a decorator would be interesting careers, or would it be better to be a schoolteacher but considered teaching English too much work because she would have to go back to college to get a master's. With a frustrated huff, she couldn't see the rush to do any of it.

Feeling whimsical and free, and skeptical and anxious to be on her own, she dreaded going to Belize to see ruins that didn't much matter to her without her friends and returned to the harbor. Browsing the ferry schedule, she bought a ticket for an island eighteen miles off the coastline. Under the island name on the ticket board, it read small and population sparse. To be "far away from the madding crowds." She smiled. She wasn't sure why she wanted quiet, but it just seemed like the best thing to have. Besides, island life reeked of romance (even if she wasn't into it), intrigue, sand, and sun.

The sky clear, not a ripple in the dark blue bay, Lucy went aboard and settled into a seat next to several other locals, many with wide-eyed babies on their laps and bundles tucked close to their feet, tattered bags and cardboard boxes filled with various goods: clothing, food staples, a microwave. She couldn't help but wonder why a cluster of attendants were stationed by several trash bins. Paper towels in their hands, they appeared to be waiting for 'something.'

*****

The 'something' on the small ship had become apparent the minute they left the harbor. A tempest was taking place in the open ocean. When the boat finally docked at the island, there was a consensual groan of relief from all the passengers. The ride had been rough. The middle passage had been filled with wild waves and wind that seemed to have come out of nowhere. The lined-up trash barrels were for people to upchuck into. The paper towels were handed out to clean the vomit from faces and the floor. Lucy had kept her stomach calmed by stepping out of the interior of the small ship and into the fervent spray of the incoming waves. She gulped the cool air in and stood sideways, riding the leaps and dips like a one-wheel hoverboard.

Once docked, she slung her backpack over her shoulder and walked off the boat. Her mind raced from the fervent trip and her capricious decision to go it alone. She didn't have a guidebook and was stumped about what to do next. The locals with their goods stumbled off the boat and stepped around her. She straightened herself out by wiping her mouth, then brushed down her shorts and stretched her legs. In awe of the tranquility of the island's inner harbor, she wondered where the tempest had gone. The ocean beyond the gut displayed a blue sky, the light dimming as the day neared evening. She watched flocks of flying birds glide by wisps of cirrus clouds; the earlier bluster was nowhere to be seen.

She took her sweater off. The heat and humidity, similar to a boiling pot of water, had zapped her last bit of energy. Her throat warbled and she cleared it by taking a sip of her tepid water, gagged, and spat it out—it reminded her of thin-runny-uncooked eggs or what they might taste like since she had never had eggs that way before.

When a group of Israelis got off, Lucy saw they were young like her, possibly early twenties. There were five of them. They wiped their mouths with scarves and the backs of their hands. They looked miserable and excited at the same time and scooted past like a wave of tumbleweeds and seemed to not notice her standing there. Lucy followed them. Phlegm squeezed her throat, and her cheeks pulled taut; her tongue tasted like putty. She slowly made her way down the dock and watched the Israelis scramble, knobby-kneed and hunched, up the hard dirt and sand embankment to a building with a large cage in front of it and a sign that read *Juanita's Tienda.*

Halfway up the embankment, she glanced around at the terrain of her new environment. A white-shelled road that passed by several Caribbean-colored houses on stilts lined the bay. It was where the shrubbery grew greener. Mangroves, palms, and fruit trees dappled and cluttered the bay's beach. The sandy knoll lay ahead, nearly barren with only a few beat-up bushes, wind-swept grasses, and three sad-looking buildings. The building with the birdcage was two stories high. It had been built with clapboard and painted white. A lopsided roof made with uneven tin was shored up the weathered palm leaves. About fifty feet to the left, a lean-to with a large maroon sign read *Milly's Gin y Cerveza.* Another smaller sign said *Today's Special: Conch Soup.* She liked conch soup, but at the moment the thought of chewy seafood and creamy water churned her stomach and told her,

"Not now."

At the bar sat two white people, a boy and a girl. They wore sandals and loose shorts and T-shirts. They were sitting with their upper bodies in the shadows and their legs in the sun. They appeared to be staring at her. Behind them stood a Carib woman with tufts of tight curls bundled into a bright green scarf. She rested her elbows and large tits on the counter; from the tilt of her head, Lucy gathered she was staring at her, too. Lucy didn't know it at the time, but the white boy and girl were Freddy and Lyla, the black woman, Milly, the owner of the establishment. They were trying to guess her nationality and whether she was cool or a goober.

Next door to the place, a few yards away, was a one-room church. Small and painted white with a light blue door, it was called *CHURCH FOR THE REDEEMED*. Lucy wondered what that meant.

Heading toward the store, before entering, she stopped to say hello to the gold and blue macaw that sat in a cage fit for a large dog or a small pony.

"Hello, bird," Lucy said, her voice scratchy from nausea and lack of talking.

The bird cocked its head and said, "*Liliady, don* take another *stop.*" The bird had the native Creole accent. Lucy laughed. She knew macaws could talk but always thought they were bad at it. It was then that the Israelis came bursting out, bags of chips and seltzer waters in their hands. The boy who had bumped into her earlier, thin with mopish black hair, stopped and tweaked Lucy's cheek. "See you later. There's only one place to get dinner. The Porch Bar and Grill." He blew her a kiss and bounded off to catch up with his friends, all legs, hair, and arms. Lucy had said nothing back but was happy to have dinner with them and entered the store.

The place sold items such as pots and pans, tablecloths, candles, cleaning fluids, canned goods, staples such as rice, beans, pasta, maize, and oodles of other sundries, along with fruit filling bins and shelves. A bored-looking dark-skinned man in his thirties sat behind the counter eyeballing her every move. He had red-rimmed, mirrored sunglasses on and smoked a cigar. His colorful button-down, short-sleeve shirt had its sleeves rolled up and exposed thin but muscled arms. She said, "Hola."

Silence. He then followed up with, "Hello."

Lucy went over to a refrigerator with glass doors and took out a bottle of soda water. She opened it and gulped a third down and burped. Screwing the top back on, she strolled over to the fruit bins and picked up a papaya to examine it. The man for some reason whistled. She looked toward the counter. He had gotten up and was coming toward her, his swagger exaggerated and amusing. It resembled a ruffian's sashay: rhythmic and lawless. The cigar pinched between his fingers produced curls of blue smoke that swirled around his body.

Once in front of Lucy, he put his hands on his hips and introduced himself as the island's *Don Juan*, even though his name was Arnoldo. A good-looking fellow, he was most likely right, she assumed and congratulated him. He was tall and had obvious strength coupled with roundish cheeks, an angled nose, and a square jawline. His features made her think of the pictures of the Tawahka men she and her friends had seen when reading about the Anthropological Reserve. Lucy pushed her light brown hair off her face. She fancied herself to have a complementary combination of features, too: her Irish, Norman, and Anglo ancestry was the reason for her thin and narrow build, while the Saxon side gave her a sturdy constitution.

Arnoldo tilted his head and puckered his full lips, then withdrew them into his mouth and smacked them together one more time. His shirt, red-flowered, green with gold, had only been buttoned up to his navel. A thick gold chain with a gold weed charm on it lay flat on his hairless chest. Lucy waited for him to say something and found her eyes zeroing in on his crotch. His brown polyester pants were overly taut and smushing a pudgy pecker against his leg. He caught her gaze and smiled. He then clapped his hands together as though enough pecker-staring had taken place (or he would charge her for the pleasure). Lucy blushed and darted her eyes at the fruit bins.

Still smiling, as if he had won something, he shifted his legs, which tucked his ostentatious member away, and began to explain how to buy the perfect papaya for immediate eating. Lucy wasn't sure what to think of him. Either an outrageous pervert or just odd. She sipped her bubbly water and waited. With a confident deep voice, he described the characteristics of a "Ripe, tasty, engorged fruit for beautiful mastication." Energy high, he tossed his sunglasses and the papaya aside and threw himself into a dance of 'fruit love.' Or at least, that is how Lucy saw it. The cantaloupes he squeezed with both hands, molding his fingers around them as he groaned with each inhalation of their scent. He caressed the sugar bananas against his hairless cheeks and rolled them around his forehead and the dark stubble of his chin. When he brought the bananas up to his lips, he let them rest against his tongue, giving each one a flick.

"*Ahan*, you must wait a day before eating these bananas, unless you can't wait," he said. Breathy, the effluence of sweet tobacco from his smoldering cigar whirled around them; he held the fruit toward Lucy for her to take.

But since it was a papaya that she wanted, he reluctantly placed the yellow but slightly green fruit back into their wooden bin. Without skipping a sensuous beat, he bent over, and with his small buttocks protruding into the air, he placed his face against each of the four papayas and proceeded to make bubbling noises as though blowing into soft flesh, then abruptly stood up. In his hand, he had a bruised one-foot fruit, glistening with juice. A chunk had been bitten out, revealing its salmon-pink innards. He handed the papaya to her, and she took it.

Lucy noticed he was sweating, and his dark cheeks were flushed. He haphazardly chewed the bitten-off rind in his mouth and swallowed. He turned and walked back to the counter. His swagger had become more of an unsteady walk than a confident stroll. Lucy found the man to be a caricature of a caricature and felt bewildered. She wondered if there was another store to buy fruit in, and then at the same time, when she looked down at the bananas, oranges, avocados, lemons, and papayas, she thumped her jaw and thought if she upped her enthusiasm for fruit, maybe she, too, could find shopping orgasmic.

Arnoldo sat once again behind the counter. He cleaned his sunglasses with a rag and placed them back on his face, then picked up a pencil, tapped loudly on the metal register, and said, "Water *sin gas*? You want the name brands, not the local. The bottle workers in Tegucigalpa piss in the bottles while they work."

Lucy glanced over the gallon-size bottles of imported water. They were three times the price. She hesitated and tried to guess if the store owner was just trying to rip her off. Unable to determine what was what, and not wanting to drink piss, she grabbed the imported. She then placed all her items on the counter: potato chips, a bitten papaya, water with and without gas, and a can of nuts. The man tallied up the cost on a piece of paper while mindlessly relighting his cigar. The cigar had the same shape as his dingdong, Lucy thought and smiled but then thought he may call out her silly grin and shut it down. She paid for her items, placed them into her daypack, and went to leave. "Stop. *Hislittle hisady*. What is your name? And where are you from?"

Lucy beamed. She liked it when people couldn't guess what nationality she was. For the past week, while spending time in La Ceiba, she had been speaking Spanish with a French accent and told people she was French Canadian, "*Je suis Quebecois*."

"Ha-ha—and I'm the King of England."

Lucy sucked on the side of her mouth. If she was going to tell people she was French Canadian, she needed to speak French or maybe just work on a better accent.

He then gave her a knowing look. "American, hey?"

"How?"

"Your features. Nooo—your accent. Features tell your ancestry, that's all. Eh, come to think of it, maybe it's the tilt of that pretty head of yours."

Lucy stared at him. She had said only two words, so it wasn't her accent. "Is there a place that cuts hair here?" It had to be her hair.

"I cut hair. Don' worry. If you want to be French, I can cut your hair French-like."

Lucy frowned and wondered what a French hairstyle would be in his mind. "Never mind," she said.

To the side of the cash register stood a bottle of gin and a couple of shot glasses. He poured himself a jigger of gin and one for Lucy. "Let's toast to your first day on the island." He handed her a cigar too, placing it on the counter with the gin shot. Lucy looked at both and reached for neither. "Why do you think it's my first day?"

"I know everyone here. And this is your first day."

"Yeah, you're right." Her earlier nausea was still clanging at her gut. A shot would settle it, she thought. And what harm could a cigar be, not that she'd ever thought of smoking one before. She picked up the gin and took a tiny sip and said, "I'm Lucy."

"As, I told you, I'm Arnoldo," he said and winked, then added, "Lucy the American who wants to be French. Tsk...tsk. Well, I'm a Carib that loves being Carib. So, how long you been in Honduras?" He picked up his drink, raised it to her, and drank the lot of it.

"Three weeks or so," Lucy said. Then seeing a stool by the counter, she sat and continued to take tiny sips of her drink. "I came with two friends, but they had to go home." She then looked out the open door. The sky was dark with traces of pink. Not having lodging yet, Lucy felt uneasy about the pressing night. Possibly he could tell her the best place to stay, she thought, even though he was a bit of a kook.

Arnoldo lit her cigar for her and leaned back against the wall. "*LiliLucy*, guess what?" Not waiting for her to guess, he continued. "I'm the richest man on this island. *Nuguya smary, gran jefe, grand homme*—I'm multilingual. Ahhh...but I don't let anything go to my head. I haven't always been rich. Eh, I've always been smart. You know, this country is agrarian—poor. Most people eat dirt three times a day. And thank the Lord for the end of the eighties. Your man Reagan and his Contra crap killed a lot of people here. Hell, we aren't Nicaragua. No...no, but everyone has to suffer, eh." His mind seemed to wander and a sadness crossed through his eyes. Abruptly, he refocused and smiled. "No worries."

Lucy puffed on the cigar and found she liked the bitter flavor. The gin's bite cleared the aftertaste; the two were a great combination. She only caught half of what Arnoldo had just said because she didn't like politics. She twisted in her seat, not sure what to say back. It wasn't the first time during her travels that someone had mentioned the United States meddling in their country's affairs, and it never seemed to be in a good way. Shrugging, she pursed her lips, feeling the gin swelling her brain. She cleared her throat. "Politics bore me." Then she smiled and took another tiny sip. She didn't know who the president of Honduras was and hoped Arnoldo wouldn't ask her. Needing salt for her stomach, she reached into her bag and took out the potato chips. She offered Arnoldo some before diving in. He took one and refilled his glass and sniffed at Lucy's drink. It was still almost half-full. He raised an eyebrow as though to say it was shameful to drink so daintily. Then said, "American. Tsk...tsk. Money grows on trees there, yah?"

"Haven't seen it. But maybe," Lucy replied.

Arnoldo laughed and slapped his knee. "Well, what do you think of the best banana republic in the world? The original and only banana republic, no matter what all the other doo-doo-head countries claim. You know why I came here?" Again, he didn't wait for a response before continuing. "My wife died suddenly. I think she ate something bad. I became depressed. She was a fun, good-looking woman. Not a good temper, though. Eh, maybe her temper killed her." He paused as if to think over other possibilities of how she may have died, then shrugged and looked at Lucy. "So, I gathered together all that mattered to me, my daughter, my bird, and donkey, and what little monies I possessed. I knew this island. Quiet, hot, and sultry, especially when the wind comes in from the west. Yah, *mon*, a good place. Perfect."

"Sorry about your wife," Lucy said and looked out the open door again. It had become night, and she kneaded her brow.

As though reading her mind, he said, "*Don'* worry, this is a safe place. Too small to kill anybody and get away with it. So, why bother?" Arnoldo paused here to puff and pour himself another gin. "Hey—hey, the devil never sleeps, though, eh?"

"What does that mean?" Lucy asked. She put a chip in her mouth and looked at him, then washed it down with the last dribble of gin. When he didn't respond, she reached into her daypack, pulled a flashlight out, and turned it on, then off, and put it in the outside webbing for easy retrieval.

"I sell batteries for cheap," he said. "But yah, every once in a while, a devil do show up."

"What does it look like?" She picked up her daypack to leave.

"Like a neighbor, a friend, a porcupine, a dog." Arnoldo didn't smile when he said this. Lucy was under the impression that whatever was whirling around in his head—a memory, a thought, his imagination gone wild—bothered him. He looked pensive, eyes remote and quiet. But then he tapped his lower lip with his index finger and laughed, a loud laugh that made Lucy jump back like he had burst out of a box. His laughter lasted a few seconds, and then he sighed. "The only place to stay is the rooming house on the beach. Ernesto's place. Fat man from the States. Honduran, though. Came here four years ago, I think. He's okay. *Don* interrupt his dinner, though." He took a sip of his drink and looked out the door. "So, diving? Sure, you are... everyone comes here to dive. Josey Wales. He's a new instructor. The last one popped his lungs out. Embolism. Had to go back to France. But Josey, maybe he'll do the same thing. He's quiet. Some think he is handsome. Eh, I'm handsomer...better personality." He said these last words while pointing at his chest. He then laughed, shifted in his seat, and leaned back against the wall. "*Lililady*, it's only a ten-minute walk to Ernesto's...*don* worry." He leaned over and poured her shot glass half full. "You drink like a mouse, so here is a mouse sip."

Lucy chuckled. "Okay." Her cigar almost out, she took three quick puffs to bring it back to life and put her pack down by her feet.

"So, as my wonderful tale of success goes, the island lacked a store. I went back to the mainland and scavenged the dump for tin for a roof and found four windows. With the few lempiras I had left, I bought supplies." He paused, his eyes searching Lucy's for what she assumed he wanted, acknowledgment for a deed well done. She nodded her approval.

"You know," he continued, "the people are happy I'm here. Before my store, soap and tinned goods were sold door-to-door by old ladies with baskets on their heads. Their supplies were unreliable and often as old as the women. I'm not cruel, though; there is still plenty of business for the skilled soap makers, coconut bread bakers, and basket weavers. You'll see them and hear them shouting their wares." He puffed and smiled. "These babies are tasty. You know I'm the richest man on the island? Can't get gas without me."

"I thought there weren't any cars here?" Lucy said.

"Lots and lots of boats. And the Aussies have a car. They drive to town to get goods from the boats and me. The Aussies also have a radio and so does Milly next door. She won't let you use her radio. If you need to call home...ask the Aussies. It's not free, though." Lucy thought she would write her parents instead of calling them. She didn't want them to try to convince her to come home.

Arnoldo gulped his shot and poured another. "I have a dirt bike," he said, continuing. "I own the diesel station on the dock. A bit like the mayor here too. No one does much without me. Eh, what do you think? Pretty big man."

Lucy smiled. The idea of a clown running the island seemed appealing. It was then that his daughter Juanita entered the store towing Bob the donkey and babbling about Fabio wanting an orange. Juanita, a chubby-faced, brown-eyed youngster nearing her middle school years had an affable imagination. She said Bob was her uncle from her mother's side of the family and claimed the bird, Fabio, was her younger brother. She went on to say that Fabio told her bedtime stories at night and sang sonorous lullabies that soothed her to sleep. Lucy thought this was plausible and loved the idea of having a bird talk and sing to her. Juanita explained, "I don't think you will ever find another Fabio. He is taller than a goat, and when he spreads his wings, he resembles a dragon."

Juanita, to Arnoldo's disapproval, took Lucy away from him. They went outside to see Fabio. "He stays outside during the day. Talks to everyone," she said. Juanita and Lucy thought it would be grand to see Fabio in flight, but then he might not come back.

The small, exotic family had wanted her to stay for dinner. Lucy thanked them but mumbled something about wanting to get settled, although what she wanted was to see what The Porch Bar and Grill had to offer. She walked out into the night, her backpack heavier; her mind felt simple from her drink and a half. Passing the Gin Y Cerveza joint, she noticed it was closed. Standing by the CHURCH FOR THE REDEEMED, she stared at its quiet fortitude, the white paint, neon in the moonlight. When she walked closer, she saw a small sign. This one was hand painted. It said, *SCHOOL, 7-11 all week long.* "A one-room schoolhouse. And the kids go every day. Yuck," she mumbled, then turned to look at the bay. The moon across the way was nearly full. It caused the sand on the beach to be white and the black water to sparkle. Not a speck of wind. The small fishing rigs were moored and still; it was picture perfect. She looked at the houses along the road and noticed most had lights on. She could hear laughter and the distant beat of reggae music being played. *How lovely*, she thought, and set off down the road, not bothering to retrieve her flashlight since the moon did a fine job illuminating the way.

When she walked by the houses, she glanced in the windows. Glassless and screenless, she could see people eating, while others played cards, and a few just stared straight ahead. Wafts of corn and coconut momentarily filled the air, making her hungry. She was glad she had come to the island. Although Arnoldo was odd, she liked his daughter, Bob, and Fabio. She also came to the realization she was completely on her own. She could do anything she wanted and thought to live in the moment because at the moment she was off to have dinner with new acquaintances, which seemed absolutely perfect.

Chapter
6

The Main Road

Lucy and Freddy walked out of the front of the Beach House to the road. They had changed into clothes for their hike to Squash Beach. Freddy had on olive-green cargo pants that were too small for his waist and too loose for his hips, so they hung low. When he bent over, his butt-crack showed. Lucy told him he should buy a belt, but Freddy felt island life shouldn't have restrictions. On his feet, he had sloppy-looking sneakers. Lucy often thought they had to smell, but since she couldn't detect any foot odor, she kept her thoughts to herself.

Lucy's sneakers had come with a Scooby-Doo figure on the toes, but the character had worn down to only Scooby's belly. She had bought the sneakers in an outdoor market in La Ceiba because her original footwear had become wet and never wanted to dry. Her snug-fitting mint-colored tank top, another recent purchase, rested across her rather flat but firm chest; the coolness of the pastel complemented her soft features. She wasn't wearing a bra. Instead, she wore a bathing suit top, the straps were tied around her neck. Her shorts, relaxed and slightly too big, were off-white terrycloth with a tied waist.

When she reached for her daypack or bent over, she often exposed her taut stomach or back or both. Although Freddy acknowledged to Lucy that she was an attractive female, he also pointed out that she wasn't his type. Lyla, a meaty Australian with copper-red hair, freckles, and blue eyes that sparkled, someone like himself, was what he preferred. Lucy had not been offended by his comment. It made perfectly good sense to her that Lyla and Freddy were an item. They looked alike. This belied a love for himself, something Lucy felt he wasn't aware of and not a subject she wanted to mention to him, either. To Lucy, Freddy was a companion, nothing more, nothing less.

Lucy's facial complexion was free of blemishes, and she wanted to keep it that way. When walking in the sun, she held an umbrella over her head. The umbrella she had was fuchsia. She felt it applauded her light-brown eyes and hair and gave her cheeks a rosy glow. Freddy, on the other hand, had a dented straw vaquero hat on. It made him look like a destitute cowboy. While walking, they were having a conversation about various people who had come to the island and left. Lucy sighed. "My first night, I had grouper at The Porch Bar and Grill with a bunch of fellows from Israel; they invited me to work on a kibbutz."

"And?"

"Possibly," she replied, then twisted her lips into distaste. "No, I don't think so, but maybe. No, okay, possibly." Slumping into an indecisive *humph*, she gave a slight chuckle. "The air smells nice here."

"I prefer swimming to digging ditches," Freddy said, giving Lucy the final nod for a possible no, but since she was unable to decide, she left the thought open for a future going-over.

The road made an unshaded shot to the town center. The terrain was filled with stunted trees, broad leaves, cacti, and flowers. The smell of earth, rot, and sweet petals waxed and waned with each step. The ground, rutty, the road consisting of only one lane, was speckled with dirt, rocks, and shells that crunched under their footfalls. The mid-morning sun, like a ball of fire, leaned on them with penetrating annoyance. Freddy stopped to wipe his brow, while Lucy took her water out of her daypack to sip on.

"One could never sneak up on anyone on this road," Lucy loudly whispered.

"Only in a crowd," Freddy smiled.

"No crowds here," Lucy stated, kicking a small pebble into the weeds.

"Peaceful."

"Do you think there is a seedy side?"

"Every place has a seedy side." Looking back around at the distant jungle, he added, "I bet there's a lot of bonking and killing going on in there. You know, between the birds and the monkeys."

Lucy laughed, a light short lift into the air. Freddy followed with a deeper laugh, more like a thrumming, cavernous bellow.

Once at the colorful houses elevated off the ground by spindly, two-by-four wooden posts, they stopped again. Ever since they had made the trek from the beach house to the fruit store, for the two days they had been hanging out together, Lucy and Freddy always stopped at the same place to comment. The stilt houses fascinated them. Painted in different coral hues, they displayed various shades of pinks, dark and bitten, bright greens, aqua blues, sun yellows, and purples from violet to almost black. The stairs that led up to the first floor, the only floor, were often strangely warped. Each house had a porch looking over the harbor and inner bay. The occupants had views of the sun setting and rising, which Freddy and Lucy both thought marvelous. Some of the roofs were tin, while others were tar paper, tiled, or a little bit of everything. Palm trees, clams, shells, and rocks made up their yards, along with the incoming tide.

"Looks like a Matisse painting but with earwigs," Lucy said, noticing the rot around the wooden posts and unrecognizable bugs worming their way in and out of holes.

"Water beetles. And centipedes," Freddy remarked and pointed at a pink house. "I like that one. I'd like to live in a pink house." An elderly woman was in a window that lacked glass or a screen. The yellowish curtains, often drawn at night for sleeping, followed her movements as she walked from one side of the room to the other.

"I think she's trying to get away from the flies," Freddy commented.

"I have a fly in my room. We're friends," Lucy said, watching the woman and the curtain.

Freddy twisted around toward Lucy, giving her a puzzled glance. "What do you call this fly friend?"

"Fly," Lucy said, her eyes glinting with humor.

Freddy picked at his fingernails, then chuckled. "I don't know if I would want a fly for a friend. All that buzzing."

Lucy looked off toward the low bushes to hide her playful grin, then looked back at the pink house. The woman was now standing in the window peering out at them. Lucy waved to her. The woman waved back, her hair frizzy white, her face looped with round, puffy circles, skin dark in areas and light on the cheeks. Her head was centered in between thin shoulders and looked wobbly. Her flat eyes appeared indifferent. When she folded back into the shadows, she disappeared. Lucy said to Freddy, "Her name is Florence. She cooks for Arnoldo and Juanita a few days a week. Cleans too. She's a friend. So, let's see, that makes...six local friends."

Freddy puckered his cheeks and made an *O* mouth. In the quiet mumblings of the last words spoken, when a small green toad hopped near him, he picked it up. "His name's José. He's my friend."

Lucy smiled. "It's about time you made a local friend."

Freddy let the toad go. Huffing, he sputtered, "Milly's a friend and not on your list. Although I could claim all of your friends, except the fly. I don't want a fly as a friend."

"I forgot about Milly. She's a friend."

An odd gurgling sound came out of Freddy. He cleared his throat, and pointedly said, "You can't just claim a friend because I say the person's a frie—"

Interrupting Freddy came the loud, long blast of the ferry's horn. It reverberated through the air and caught them off guard. "It's Sunday. The ferry doesn't come until midafternoon on Sundays," he snuffled.

They both looked out into the bay. There was no sight of an incoming small ship. What they saw were kids around five or six jumping off the long dock that held the common toilet, an outhouse for the people who lived in the colorful houses. The toilet's exterior was painted aqua blue, and the roof had been matted with palm leaves. A bow-legged man held a book, reading it while he walked out the door, its springlike hinges slamming it shut, catching and holding Freddy and

Lucy's attention. When the man walked by the kids, who were readying themselves to jump, he patted and goofed with their hair, making remarks that neither Freddy nor Lucy could hear.

"Do you think he just wiped his hands on their heads?" Lucy said.

"Gross."

Before they could make another comment, they were disrupted again by the booming horn of the ferry. They looked around once more for the white behemoth boat with a red steering house, but it was nowhere in sight. The horn kept blaring, causing Freddy to cringe. When it stopped, they looked at each other astonished that the sound was so loud. It had never been that loud before.

"It's so close," Lucy said, staring down the road to the other side of the bay.

Freddy gazed toward the horizon. "Not a cloud in the sky."

"Look, the mailboat. It's amazing that soggy, beaten-up hunk of wood makes it here with all those waves," Lucy said, gazing at the misfit vessel as it grumbled through the mouth of the harbor.

"Probably why the mail's always wet."

"I don't think it has a horn," Lucy said.

"It has a bell. The fellow—what's his name, Juan?—he rings it once parked at the dock. It's a pretty, light sound. Not this racket."

The heavy wooden mail boat lugged while the engine made groaning noises each time it pushed through a swell. Bags of mail were piled toward the back, and a dark-haired woman was standing on the port side looking out. The sun lit her face. She was white and wore dark sunglasses. Her hands on the rail, she appeared to be looking straight at them. They waved at her; she waved back.

"A foreigner. How many others do you think on the boat?" Lucy inquired.

"Usually two or three."

"What nationality?"

"Too far away."

"I think she's French."

"I say Greek." Freddy looked at Lucy and held out his hand. "I bet a pilito."

They shook hands.

The ferry horn blared again. Once more, they both looked down at the harbor and to the east, then west, but the only moving object was the mail boat. It was now being skillfully turned into the ferry dock. "You're right, it's not the mail boat. The sound's coming from someplace else," Lucy said. The ferry horn, which had stopped blasting, began again. This time Lucy looked over toward the sandy knoll where the store stood. The sun baking the earth made the store, gin bar, and church wavy and surreal. Squinting, she burst out laughing and grabbed Freddy's shirt tails. "Hurry, I know what it is." They scrambled along with Freddy, at first trying to peddle backward away from Lucy's grip, but when he caught on, he laughed, "Why of course." Lucy let him go, and they skipped forward into a clumsy run. After a few seconds, they stopped to catch their breath and petered back into their normal, and very comfortable, slow walk.

Fabio was in his usual place, in his cage right outside the store doorway. As they neared the store, they watched him open his mouth and crane his head into the air. The ferry sound shook the ground. "He's making the noise. How funny," Lucy shouted over the siren, beaming like a proud mother.

It was then that Arnoldo came charging out the door. He hit the cage with a flat, straw broom while berating the bird. Both Lucy and Freddy stared at his pudgy pecker. When he stomped the ground, it didn't move. He ran back into the store as though a phone was ringing, only it wasn't.

"That was not nice," Freddy sniped. "And that penis of his. Makes me feel inferior." Scrunching his mouth toward his nose, he continued, slipping a sly glance toward Lucy, "My friend Milly likes him."

"I know," Lucy replied. Her expression, smug. "My good friend Milly told me. But he's not interested."

"Really?" Realizing he should have kept quiet, he frowned, followed by a frumpy huff. Once they were standing in front of the cage, Fabio looked at them with a cocked head. Freddy pointed his finger at Fabio while looking at Lucy, insisting, "Have it say my name." He then smiled as though proud of himself for taking control of the situation.

Freddy's puffery caused Lucy to giggle, but she bit her lower lip to stop herself and asked, stifling a smile, "What's your name?" When Freddy wouldn't answer, she said, "Your real name."

"I want the bird to say Freddy."

"Why Freddy?"

"Freddy is my name."

"Really, Freddy?

"Yes, Freddy."

Lucy opened the palm of her right hand. Somehow during their walk or possibly when they had approached Fabio, she had put a peeled sugar banana in her right hand. Since it was the size of an adult pinkie, she had hidden it easily. Holding it up in front of the bird, she said, "Freddy."

"Freeeeddddy!" the parrot sang into the air like a two-bit actor. Lucy put the fruit in between the bars, and Fabio darted forward, nabbed it with his beak, and gulped it down.

"You owe me a pilito—-Freeeeddddy," Lucy said, mimicking the parrot's voice.

"Why did he sing my name? You didn't sing it."

"He likes to have fun."

"Yesterday, I don't recall you giving him food," Freddy said, miffed because he felt duped. He also was staring at Fabio as though a child's science experiment gone awry. Shrugging, Freddy reached into his fanny pack sifting around for a pilito. Having found one, he handed the tiny, weightless coin to Lucy, her expression a smirk about to burst into laughter. "You look like the cat that swallowed the canary," Freddy remarked.

Lucy, still grinning, cleared her throat and explained, "I've been teaching him my name since I met him. I didn't have time to practice yours."

Looking Lucy up and down, Freddy asked, "So, where do you keep the sugar bananas?"

Lucy pulled a bunch of the small bananas out of her fanny pack.

A limp, empty peel was still attached to the three others.

"Is this what you do back home? Train birds?"

"No, but it could be fun."

"Probably not if you do it for a living."

Lucy looked askew at Freddy then off toward the bay. Deep in thought over the possibilities for a career, she went through her usual list of ideas such as being an interior decorator, lawyer, street vendor, painter, then bit down on her lower lip. "I think bird trainer has potential."

"Okay, but today we are looking for a lost spring, which makes us—in Danish we call it *leder efter vand med en pind*."

"You've never spoken to me in Danish. I like it."

"You're not going to be Danish now?"

"No, Danish is too foreign."

"What? Anyway, looking for water with a stick," Freddy said, his mouth flat, pressed against his teeth.

"Dowsing."

"That's it."

"That's fun. Yes, happy-go-lucky dowsers," Lucy said, her eyes wide and bubbly.

Then they both laughed stupidly, which made them laugh for real. And Fabio joined them.

Chapter
7

The Folder

Early morning, the docks at the Coxen Hole marina in Roatan were alive with activity. Fishermen headed out, commercial boats came in, and sightseeing tour guides waited patiently with clipboards and wearing baseball caps, for their clients. The mail boat sat quietly against the main dock. The fenders squeaked with every minuscule roll. Old wood painted, sanded, and repainted a hundred times caused the hull to be thick and lumpy white. Once a lobster boat used by a northern fast-food chain, it became the Bay Island mail boat after a storm ripped it away from its mooring. Eventually discovered in one of the island's coves by the Honduran Coast Guard, the boat became the property of the country.

Eleanor was in the pilothouse. An American woman in her early thirties, she was pretty, athletic, and spoke fluent Spanish; it had been a goal of hers to learn the language. Having gone to language schools in Mexico, she had also worked in an orphanage in Guatemala. Before working for the Honduran government as a mailwoman, she lived in Panama for several months scuba diving. It was there that she earned her Divemaster certificate, and her ability to speak the native language had finally fallen into place. In between Panama and her job, she had flown home to the States to take the language test at the college she had attended years prior to traveling. She passed the exam and received her university diploma. She felt she now had better choices in life and chose to become a scuba diving instructor and flew to the sunny shores of Roatan, Honduras. With its clear water, coral reefs, and soft currents, diving aficionados flocked to the place. Several dive shops lined the west end, and Eleanor had hoped to get an instructor job. But apparently, others thought to do the same thing, and there was a glut of willing workers and no jobs. For the time being, delivering the mail was fine.

Eleanor sat on a swivel chair in the mail boat's pilot house and waited for Captain Juan to return from town with a paying passenger. It was something they did for extra money, ferrying people, pets, and other items (along with the mail) back and forth from the islands and the mainland. Juan had told her the passenger was male, foreign, and wealthy. Possibly he would tip them well, she thought with a smile.

The windows open, a comfortable breeze brushed her face as she read a *Vogue* magazine Juan's wife had given her when eating breakfast. It was the Hispanic edition. Women were big-boobed and big-bottomed, big-haired, wearing lots of lipstick, and most were blonde. Flipping to the horoscope page, she read under Virgo, "Be open-minded this month; life will be full of opportunities." She smiled. *Maybe that dive instructor job will come my way.*

Hearing Juan's voice, she looked up. Out the window, she could see him and another man walking down the dock. The man was tall and lanky with a relaxed stride, arms swinging, and head lofty. He was looking toward the sky as though singing. The man also caused Juan to look very short, but then Juan *was* short. His wife was short too. Both were in their seventies, bent, but hardy, with gray and white hair and wrinkles that flourished like well-worn shoe leather. Eleanor had met them because she was a friend of one of their daughters. The daughter, Julia, had a cookout in La Ceiba a month ago, which Eleanor had attended. Juan had hurt his back, so his wife suggested Eleanor, in need of work, should become his mail assistant. She also, matter-of-factly, told her, "Hanky-panky with girls wasn't his thing," and asked Eleanor to keep an eye on him if he came across a cute man.

Juan took the passenger's duffel and put it on the floor of the cockpit. The man wouldn't give up his black attaché, which was slung over a shoulder, nor the paper bag he had with what looked like a bottle of something. Having gone out to help them, Eleanor offered the fellow her hand so he could step into the boat more securely, but Juan told her he would handle it. He not only took the man's hand but folded his buttery, fat fingers around his waist and with the other hand, pinched a chunk of his buttocks while apologizing for the rough surf. With barely an ounce of wind, his sentiments were absurd. The scene made Eleanor laugh to herself and shake her head with the frivolity of disbelief. She had been told about his dalliances with men, but this was the first time he had been so overt.

The passenger looked no more than forty. He wore neatly pressed pistachio-colored LL Bean shorts and a beige, short-sleeved polo shirt. He had a boyish flare and handsome lines to his face; his white skin was lightly tanned by the sun. His light-brown hair was dappled with blond streaks and neatly coiffed around his ears. His bangs were brushed back. His steely-blue eyes and firm lipless mouth appeared whimsical and possibly shrouding a temper. He slapped Juan's hand away from his bottom. Juan took this opportunity to grab hold of the fellow's long fingers and hold them to his face like some lovesick teen.

"Stop that!" he shouted. His accent was similar to a southern drawl minted with British aristocracy. Eleanor wondered where he was from. The man roughly pushed Juan. Juan took it in stride but tumbled toward the pilothouse and caught the door before falling. Eleanor didn't think this was a good start to their trip to the neighboring island, but then what did it matter? They would dump the man off in an hour and most likely never see him again.

Eleanor looked at Juan for a directive. Juan heaved a disappointed sigh, then with heavy-tongued Spanish, he flatly said to their passenger, "Sit, we need to leave." To Eleanor, he whispered, "What a waste. Get him some water or beer. Charge him." He then winked at her and entered the pilothouse to start the engine.

Eleanor felt there was something not quite right about the new fellow. It had nothing to do with whether he liked Juan or not. But it did occur to her that he may be drunk. Having been told to take a seat, he began to circle like a dog searching for the best space to lie down. Eleanor chuckled at the odd man's antics and took a bottle of water out of the cooler to give to him. But when he teetered, missed the bench, and fell to the cockpit floor, landing on his bottom with his brown paper bag lifted into the air, she thought not. It appeared he had brought his own beverage. She watched him place the bag on his lap and take a half-full bottle of whiskey out. He kissed it with the same reverence Juan had displayed when fondling the man's fingers. Unscrewing the top, he engulfed a large swig, gulped, and gave a sigh that lasted for far too long. Eleanor frowned. A malaise of disappointment flooded in, but unlike Juan, who wanted him for his body, she had hoped for some interesting conversation. Juan primarily liked to talk about his mother and her hernia—a very boring subject.

Juan motioned to her from the pilothouse, and Eleanor got out of the boat to release the dock lines. She then got back on board, drew in the fenders, and left their passenger, who was now talking to himself about a man named Heraldo, and went into the pilothouse. She sat back down on the swivel chair and picked up the *Vogue* questionnaire "Finding Your Perfect Soulmate" to continue filling it out. The early morning air, malleable, had a light, lofty breeze that was almost palatable.

Once out of the harbor, the swells were mellow and glossy. Not a cloud in the sky; the sun was still low over the ocean. The sea, bird warbles, thrumming of the engine, and the warm, salty air were hypnotic. But then their passenger decided to join them.

"It's lonely out there," he said, dragging his duffel in with him. His attaché in one hand, a bottle of whiskey in the other, he reclined to the floor and leaned into his duffel. Relaxed, he put his feet onto a mailbag. "I'm Liam," he said, then looked at Eleanor and asked, "I know Juan, but who are you?"

"Eleanor." She watched him take another big gulp from his bottle. She had no desire to engage in a conversation with a drunk. Juan wasn't going to talk to him either and seemed to be pretending he didn't exist; eyes bloodshot from age and sea, he focused on the surf ahead, his ability to navigate the ocean a far cry superior to his attempts at carnal duplicity.

Liam left to his own entertainment, began to sing a song about fat girls and diddling. His vocal range was light and simple yet frequently croaked like a frog. As the boat pushed on and the more he drank, the sloppier the nonstop sexualized lyrics became. In mid-tune, he switched from singing ribald rants to muttering about his life being unfair. He bemoaned the travesty of his birth to the mailbag next to him: "I'm a middle child of three in a Chilean family that should never have had children." When Eleanor saw from the corner of her eye Liam kick the mailbag near his feet with frustration, she cleared her throat to get Juan's attention. The mailbags that they kept in the pilothouse usually contained delicate items. When Liam kicked it again, Juan said, without turning around, "The mail is more important than you. Do it again, and your trip has ended," then sighed, crestfallen that such an attractive man was a buffoon.

"Whatever," he responded like an obstinate child of twelve who had just been caught telling a lie, then quieted down but only long enough to think of what next to do with his time. With a sly twist of the month, he smacked his lips and glanced around the room, possibly to try to find something interesting to comment on. Eleanor watched boredom cross over his curious eyes since there was nothing remarkable about their early morning boat ride. Not wanting him to see her interest in his antics, Eleanor pretended to work on her questionnaire but followed his every move from the corner of her eye. He rummaged in his pocket and pulled out a packet of crumpled cigarettes. He lit one and took a hard, long draw. Something about the way he pulled on his cigarette reminded her of another. She thought of Dorian. Their relationship had lasted only a month. Although he was handsome, his spoiled nature and narcissistic tendencies, like the man presently in front of her, became too much. There was also something about Liam's eyes that matched Dorian's. It was uncanny and it bothered her, like eating a meal she'd forgotten she hated. Besides, she was in love with another. She was in love with a man she felt she would never see again, Harry Van Cleef. Why her heart remained loyal to their memories boggled her. They had last seen each other a little over a year ago, and no matter how many dates or lovers brushed her life, Harry always popped back into her thoughts. Given enough time, she groused, he will fade further and further away, which saddened her, along with being webbed with a certain hope of relief.

Liam resumed his whining, which brought Eleanor back to the present situation, a drunken client and his pathetic woes. "The worst part of being born to wealth? They didn't groom me for anything except to be a playboy." This comment caused Juan to roll his eyes at Eleanor; she did the same back to him.

After another exasperating huff, he asked, "Eleanor, are you Juan's daughter?"

A foot or so taller than Juan, her eyes were green, her hair was dark, her skin was pale, and their features dissimilar; his heavy, hers' light. "No, employee," Eleanor muttered while bending her head to read a question in the magazine: "Which do you prefer? Eating out or cooking together at home with your boyfriend?" It was difficult to answer since she liked the idea of both.

"I'm a detective," Liam said, interrupting her thoughts. "Well, I was a detective for the Johannesburg police." He took another pull off his cigarette. Leaving the cigarette to rest in the corner of his mouth, he tilted the bottle of whiskey to see how much was left. "I'll be out soon. How long until we arrive?"

Eleanor leaned back in her chair and put the magazine on the console. Liam reminded her of a mosquito buzzing around an ear. Since she couldn't slap him, she decided to engage him in conversation. Possibly he had a good detective tale. "Detective? I thought you're just a playboy," she said and fixed her eyes on him.

"Both pretend jobs for my pretend life. I even pretend to be happy. It's not working, though." His small blue eyes bore into Eleanor's as though daring her to say otherwise. Once again, Eleanor reflected on Dorian. How did this man get Dorian's eyes?

"Hell, I just wish my family would give me my inheritance early and leave me alone, but I guess it's their way of controlling me," Liam said swishing his mouth around. "I would be real once rich enough to not have worries. No more pretending. Yes, that is what that money would do for me." He leaned in, to whisper, "Don't tell anyone, but I'm on a pretend mission to capture a fellow who is pretending to be someone else." He then laughed a haughty, baritone guffaw and coughed. Seeing he needed to spit, Eleanor handed him a rag. "Thank you," he replied as he disposed of the phlegm into the oil-stained cloth. He then wiped his chin, leaving black oil marks behind on his jaw. Taking the top of the bottle, he took a sip, then continued, "I need to solve this idiotic mission to keep in good graces with the parents. Oh, anyway. Let me try something. I have a name that I want you to think about. This is for you, too, Juan. Do either one of you know a fellow called Heraldo Pinola Alvares Vander Gar de Unias? I'd say he is in his mid-thirties. Handsome." Smiling, he turned toward Juan. "Someone you might like."

Juan rolled his eyes at Eleanor again; she did the same back.

"No," Eleanor said, yet a pinch of recognition once again caught her off guard. Only this time it chilled her veins. "That's a very long name. What was it again?"

"You *do* know it?"

"That's not what I said." Eleanor sensed she had made a mistake but wasn't sure how to fix it.

"Heraldo Pinola Alvares Vander Gar de Unias," Liam repeated, then added, "He has an alias. Can't remember it, though. I have it written down." He tapped his attaché, indicating the name was in there, and smiled.

Yes, she believed that was his real name. According to the paper, *La Noticia*, Harry Van Cleef was an alias. It caused an uneasy pull to her heart and groin. *How funny*, she thought. She had just been thinking of him, and now this man was looking for him, and then again, *How odd? How strange?* That they would be ferrying a man to an obscure island off of Honduras who is on a mission to find Harry. Or was it? Her emotions, briefly unfettered, fluttered across her face.

"You do know him." Liam sat up. Her reaction seemed to sober him up.

Eleanor laughed, "No. I don't." Again, she felt she had made a mistake and tried her best to shut her inner flummox down. She wasn't positive if it was Harry's real name, Heraldo Pinola Alvares Vander Gar de Unias. It was so long, just one word out of place and the fugitive would be someone else. She went back to the magazine to finish the questionnaire. She also needed time to think, to jog her memory.

Liam became unusually quiet, and the room finally became pleasant to be in. She tried to answer the last question but could feel his penetrating eyes on her as though reading her thoughts. She ignored him to concentrate, even though it was difficult: "Do you prefer city living or country living?" She put *country*. As she added up the points, Liam's persistent stare got the better of her. She did not want to talk about the Harry/Heraldo character. She needed to move on with her life, not get sucked into an investigation. And if it were Harry, Liam was after, well, she wasn't about to say a word. In an attempt to change the subject, she said, "My perfect soulmate is a well-read older man who likes to travel." She looked directly into Liam's eyes and tossed the magazine in a trash bin under the console.

"I don't like white women; I prefer my women to have a richer, lustier color. Sorry." Liam shifted forward and knocked over his bottle of whiskey. "Oh, there you are," he said. "Good to see I put the cap back on." He then unscrewed the top and drank. "Brown liquid of joy. To think I still have more of you left." He took another. He then screwed the top on and placed the bottle on the floor. "So, Eleanor, do you have something to tell me? Something important about this Heraldo?"

"No." She looked at him exasperated, then turned away. She could see in the far distance the island they were heading for. It was just a speck. The waters were calm, clean, and blue.

"I'm not interested in hurting him. *But he's a criminal.*"

Eleanor looked at Juan. He hadn't moved his eyes, hands, or feet since they'd motored into the open ocean. He had a far-off gaze as though in another world; gone off to somewhere special, she thought. The sea had a way of capturing people and holding onto them.

"So, Eleanor, did you hear me?" She looked at Liam, and he smiled. His cigarette down to the nub, he put it out on his shoe, then lit another. "That's better. I don't like being ignored. Now, where was I? Yes, Heraldo took a large chunk of my family's money. Him and that auntie of his. What's her name? She's a Mapuche. Very independent group of people in my country."

"Country?" Eleanor questioned.

"Chile. Anyway, I know she's the one who masterminded the whole mess—it was a contract gone awry between that Mapuche auntie and my daddy. But for some reason, my parents are more interested in Heraldo. I think it's a macho thing. You know, a woman could never be that clever." He then belched and growled and put his hand up to his chin. The oil residue left from the cloth had made his chin slimy. He tried to wipe the grease off but grew tired at its stubbornness and stopped. Eleanor smiled. He then pulled on his cigarette and let the smoke exit through his nose, and like Juan, he went off somewhere in his head staring at his spent cigarette on the floor and remained silent. The thrust of the boat hitting the light surf and the moaning of the engine were all that could be heard. Then suddenly Liam tried to push his duffel and the mailbags away from him. They wouldn't budge. He was having another tantrum.

"Behave." Juan's tone, stern.

"Fine." Liam settled down and glanced from Juan to Eleanor and back again to Eleanor and asked, "You've taken him on this boat, haven't you?"

Juan spoke without turning around, "Señor, we take a lot of people on this boat. I have been doing this for twenty years. Some people we talk to. Some we don't. The name is not familiar."

"I suppose." Liam's mood turned gloomier. After a few minutes of pouting, he began to babble again. "Trust me. This family of mine needn't trash anyone else's life for anything, but of course they want more. More cars, more houses, more land, more servants... Hence, trash away Father and Mother. Hell, I suppose I take after them. I want more too." He paused to click his teeth together and burp, then continued. "I think it's due to a grudge. Señor Unias was my father's business partner. I liked the man. I liked Heraldo-Harry, whatever his name is now. I'm sure it's neither of those... He was younger than me. Sent off to boarding school in Europe when he was ten. Didn't want to go, but well. He didn't behave well. Smart fellow. He had balance for a small boy. You know, the way some people just never seemed ruffled by nuances... It drove his parents nuts how calm he would be after breaking a vase in the house or pilfering the local tienda for gum. Anyway, Ricardo, Señor Unias was a very wealthy man, and so was that half-sister of his, the Indian-Mapuche." Liam paused here, leaned back against the wall, took a small sip of whiskey, smoked, and continued. "I shouldn't be telling you all this. But, well, who cares? Guess what?" Losing focus, he drifted off somewhere. Then, as though he forgot where he was, he began to mumble something to the walls, then laughed and turned toward Eleanor. "My father was jealous. Loved the wife." He then laughed again. "Lust and desire...such a curse." Once again, he paused. He took a small sip of whiskey and slouched lower to the floor. He appeared tired and desiring to nap.

Eleanor twisted the ends of her hair and got up. She went down to the lower deck to a small room by the head. The room had a round window to the outside world that had been shut to keep the water out. Because the room was musty with a hint of mildew, she could see dust in the air. It was her bedroom. A bunk with a thin mattress and her backpack were the only items in the room.

She knelt by the pack and unzipped a side pocket. Fishing around, she found a small notebook and pulled it out. In between the pages were several newspaper articles. She shifted through them and removed two. One was about two girls being beaten to death in a mountain village, the other, was about a man found dead along a river. She tucked the article about the girls back into her notebook and unfolded the one about the man.

She let her eyes roam over the words. When she found what she was looking for, the name, Heraldo Pinola Alvares Vander Gar de Unias, she took a deep breath. She had wanted to confirm that the name was the same one Liam had mentioned, and it was. She knew the article had been wrong about his death and that he was still alive. She also assumed she would never hear or know about the man who had been her lover—the man she knew as Harry—again. The article had been kept as a memento.

She was confounded that their passenger, Liam, was looking for Harry here in Honduras. Eleanor had been under the impression that Harry had left the area. Possibly gone to Europe. She put the article away. Her fingers then touched upon another object in the pocket; she pulled it out. It was Harry's locket. That fateful day the dead body in the mangroves was mistaken for Harry's, the police had left the locket on the dock beside his confiscated bag, passports, and other items. She had taken it when they weren't looking—as another memento.

She sat back against the wooden bunk and unclipped the latch. The photos were in black and white. On one side, there was an attractive woman. She was young looking with her dark hair wrapped up on top of her head. Her brow and arch of her eyes were the same as Harry's. On the other side, a man. He had a mustache and a full head of hair, thick tufts that looked unmanageable. There was one thick curl over his forehead. His nose angled, his chin firm. Harry had his father's hair and nose. Eleanor felt sick thinking how they might have died. Then something very protective roused its way inside of her. Although she and Harry hadn't parted well, she had only hoped for the best for him. The police had found several passports with different aliases that belonged to him. She understood he had needed to leave, but what she did not understand was the reason why. What had happened that made that one night so explosive? Why had people come gunning for him and his aunt? She thought about the drunken man sitting on the pilothouse floor. He was accusing Harry of being a criminal and so had the papers. She didn't want to accept those accusations, and knowing what she knew of Central American politics: the lies, the thieving, the duplicity, the chances of Harry being a thief were most likely not true. But she wasn't sure. She had her doubts since there were so many people after him.

The hot airless room was stifling. Eleanor shrugged and got up to wipe the sweat from her brow with a towel that had been tossed on the bed. She then paused for a minute and tapped her index finger on the wall. What had Alex said? *I know where your lover is.* What did that mean? She had not thought much about it at the time. She and Alex disliked each other. One might say they were enemies when working at the orphanage together. She put Alex out of her mind and pursed her lips. *Was Harry living in Honduras? That would be stupid.*

Eleanor walked back up to the deck, took a water bottle out of the cooler, and went into the pilothouse. Liam was singing again. This time a Chilean song about goats: *the goats were in the Andes and Santiago was on fire.* She sat down on the swivel chair and threw Juan another exasperated look. He returned the same. Eleanor refocused her attention on the upcoming island. The gut to its bay was about a quarter of a mile in front of them. It was still early morning; the skies were bright and the surf soft.

"Oh, do tell, missy. Do you know the fellow?" Liam asked, interrupting his song. He seemed wide awake. "I could use all the help I can get. You see, I'd like to go fetch my mistress and escape to Tahiti."

"Stop asking. I don't know him," she snapped, keeping her eyes on the waters around the island.

"Liam Francisco de Nepomuceno María de los Remedios Titlemen de Ramos."

"Titlemen?" It wasn't a common name. And it was Dorian's last name too. She swallowed hard. The possibility that Dorian and Liam were family members was troubling, along with hideous.

"My mother, a beauty from Halifax, Nova Scotia. My father met her when at Yale. She hasn't aged well, but, well, she takes after me." He laughed and held up his bottle of whiskey, paused, pouted, then continued. "So, do you like how long my name is? I only use two, though: Liam Titlemen." He looked happy. Pleased with himself, he sighed and dug into his front pants pocket. When he found what he was looking for, he said, "Yup," and took out a key. Clumsily, he tried to open the attaché but was unable to. "I want to show you, his picture."

Astonished that he had a picture of Harry, she jumped up. "Let me help."

Liam, not wanting to let her hold the case, held it tightly between his hands as she opened it up. Once opened, he pulled the case back and placed it on his lap. Eleanor crouched beside him to peek in. His breath smelled of hot whiskey and smoke, his body of soap. She moved sideways to avoid his breath. There was a passport, money, and a few other papers, along with a folder. Liam shuffled the papers around and sloppily took the folder out. He then stared at it as though confused about what he was doing.

"Could I see?" Eleanor asked reaching for the folder At first, he resisted, but then he her have it. A tiredness had come over him again. When his face suddenly turned grayish white, he fell back hard against the wall and slumped off his duffel onto the floor. Eleanor kicked his foot. "Are you all right?"

He opened his eyes. "I feel sick."

Liam's tongue wagged and lapped at his chin. He then crawled onto his knees, hand over hand, and dragged himself out the door and onto the deck. Lifting himself up by the gunwale, he wretched over the side of the boat and remained hanging over the side. Eleanor quickly glanced at the folder. She saw the three photos of Harry, his aunt, Yena, and the boy who had driven her in his boat to the orphanage the night she had arrived at the town, so many moons ago. There were several other papers that looked like some sort of report. When Liam fell back onto the deck with a thud, she looked up. Panic struck. She wasn't sure what to do with the information in her hands. Without thinking, she shut the folder and stuffed it beneath a box under the console. She then closed the attaché and locked it—yet kept the key so he wouldn't immediately reopen it and wonder where the goods went. Juan watched her but said nothing.

Liam reentered the room, the same way he had exited, crawling. When he found his duffel, he curled up beside it and fell asleep. Ten minutes away from docking, they were happy to have the silence. Juan suggested she toss cold water from the cooler on the "jackass's" head, once docked. Eleanor gladly followed his orders and went out on the deck to get a bucket and fill it with the cooler water. The air was heavenly compared to the cramped pilothouse and its whiskey smell. She stood by the gunwale for a moment to breathe and look off at the island. Two figures, a boy and a girl, were looking at her. The girl had a pink umbrella over her head. The boy was tall and beefy. Eleanor stared back. They waved. She waved at them.

As the boat docked, she took the cooler water and splashed it onto Liam's face. He sputtered and sat up. Juan gave a chuckle while Eleanor exited to secure the ropes around the pilings. Her emotions had also gone into a tailspin. What had she just gotten herself involved in?

She deemed Liam and his criminal investigation Latin American espionage, and nothing good could come of it. *How foolish*, she thought, *or is it?* The notion of protecting Harry, a lovely gesture, but was it necessary? And was it stupid? But what was done, was done. She watched Liam muddle his way onto his feet and hoped he wouldn't remember the trip. If he did, there was always the excuse that he was so drunk, he lost his folder. But a febrile sense of angst bit her nerves as her knee-jerk reaction to take the folder began to seem dumber and dumber.

Eleanor stood on the dock with Juan as he rang the bell for Arnoldo. They both helped Liam off. They handed him his duffel. He had his attaché and bottle of whiskey already in his hands. They bid him goodbye and good luck and watched him drag his duffel as he teetered toward land, his attaché slapping his side, the bottle of whiskey tucked under his arm. Arnoldo was running down the dock to greet the group and almost knocked Liam off, but Liam caught himself before falling. Once at the end of the dock, Liam tripped and collapsed into a heap on the ground. Because he was on his back, prone, they figured he had passed out again. Juan turned to Eleanor. "What was that?"

"Something unfortunate."

"Trouble," he said while dragging a mailbag out of the boat, then added, "You better hope he doesn't remember anything." He pursed his lips. "Didn't sound right. That is, what he is doing. Cute but what a miserable man."

Juan handed Eleanor the mailbag. "I didn't think this out well," she said, a tone of regret in her voice. "When do we leave?"

"Not until tonight. I'm helping Arnoldo out with his plans for a five-star hotel on the island. Did I tell you I used to be an architect?"

"No. Fascinating," Eleanor said and picked up the mailbag.

"Yup. Lots of things are fascinating."

Arnoldo walked up to the boat out of breath. He had been running like a demented spider, arms clawing the air, legs and feet sawing the ground. Juan retrieved two beers from the boat and handed one to Arnoldo. Now pumping gas into the boat's tank, Arnoldo thanked Juan. They both sipped their beverage and watched Eleanor carry the mailbag down the dock, then shifted their gaze toward Liam. "Borracho gigante," Juan mumbled. They both looked at each other and rolled their eyes.

Chapter
8

The Greek and Josey

On their way to the store, Lucy and Freddy saw Juanita outside the back door sweeping the yard. Bob the burro stood next to her, his feet perfectly parallel, his disposition quiet yet interested. Chickens, red and black, were milling around. They pecked at the ground and occasionally at Bob, who paid no mind. Arnoldo was behind the counter picking his teeth with a toothpick. He read the paper with his dark, red-rimmed sunglasses at the tip of his nose. He looked up when they walked in. "Lucy! Stop teaching my bird crap. I don't like horns."

"I didn't teach him that." Lucy turned toward Freddy, eyeing the machetes. "I wonder if we will have to bushwhack?"

"I hope not."

Sidestepping the machetes, they walked around and looked at the boxed goods, bags of old spaghetti, and various arrays of hot sauces.

Freddy picked up a can of peanuts. He shook the can and frowned. "Barely any and pricey." He put the peanuts back. Finally, they settled on two large bottles of water (imported), a couple of oranges, and four lunch-size bags of potato chips. Placing it all on the counter, Arnoldo perused the contents, grunted, then looked up at Lucy and over to Freddy. He gave an insinuating chuckle and said to Freddy, "Hey, fast guy."

"What?" Freddy asked.

"The girl. Fast guy."

Lucy rolled her eyes. They divided up the cost equally, paid, and put the goods in their day packs. Lucy took the lion's share. She didn't want Freddy eating it all before they got to the beach.

When they stepped outside, Freddy stewed. "Just because he's a dog doesn't mean I'm one."

"Well, Lyla did just leave, and now you're with me." Although Arnoldo wasn't on her list of friends because she felt he was too peculiar, she did not think he was a complete dog, just a half-dog.

"Bye, Fabio." Lucy threw him a kiss.

Fabio squawked, straightened himself up, and whistled like a construction worker at a pretty girl.

"Takes after his owner," Freddy mumbled.

The tinkling sound of a bell could be heard, and Arnoldo charged out the door, startling all three of them. His tight pants, too high, exposed his ankles and gave him a wedgie; his small bottom, cramped and outlined. His pudgy penis looked tucked under. Fabio made a forced laugh sound, which set Lucy and Freddy doubling over with laughter.

When their giggles subsided, all three stared at Arnoldo's gangly body running down the incline and along the dock to the mail boat. The dark-haired girl they saw earlier in the bay stood on the dock talking to Juan. Juan, who was still in the boat, handed her a small backpack, along with a bag of mail. There was another man walking crookedly down the dock. When Arnoldo passed him, he almost fell into the water, but like a dexterous ballerina, he saved himself by doing a pirouette, then planted his feet steadfast onto the dock to continue his walk.

"Juan gave that woman a mailbag," Freddy said, then continued to narrate the scene. "Now he's getting out too. Now the three of them are watching the wobbly, thin man walk down the dock. He's dragging his duffel like a real sot."

Lucy's eyes widened as she watched the man drag his bag over the wooden planks. When he finally reached firm ground, he stopped to light a cigarette. "I know that man. My friends and I met in Copan," she said.

"Really?"

"A real drunk."

They watched him stumble and fall flat on his back by the water's edge. His cigarette still between his fingers, swirled little curls of smoke by his side. Like a seal, he bobbed his head as though it were going to move him along. They waited for him to get up. But he slumped back, lifeless.

"Passed out," Lucy said.

"Wow, early for that."

They turned their attention toward Arnoldo. He was now pumping gas while Juan watched. The girl was on her way down the dock with the mailbag in her arms but then put it down to drag it. When it snagged, she put it on top of her head.

"Mail," Freddy said. "Should we wait? Maybe I have a letter from Lyla."

"Small world." Lucy pointed her chin toward the dock. "I spoke to her in Le Ceiba. I can't remember her accent, but I don't think she's French or Greek. I also don't think a French woman would put a mailbag on her head either, especially if it's wet."

"A Greek would," Freddy said, looking up into the sky. "The sun says midmorning. Oh, hell. We better get going."

They walked down the road. By the dock with the public outhouse, a trawler had pulled up and Josey was getting on. "Where's he going?" Freddy said.

"I guess he's fishing today," Lucy remarked.

"Can't be. He's got a whole lotta divers here taking lessons."

Lucy ignored Freddy and walked down to the dock. She wanted to ask Josey where he was going. However, the trawler pulled away, and she was left to stand on the shoreline waving to him in hopes he would see her. But Josey was too engaged with the other men on board, Lucy walked back to Freddy and said, "I tried."

"Tried what?"

"To find out."

"Who cares? We're wasting precious time. Before we know it, it will be dark."

"I bet he's going to the mainland to get supplies," Lucy said.

"I think he's playing hooky."

They shook hands.

Wanting to make up for lost time, they skipped along for a few steps until they realized they'd gone mad again, moving so rapidly in the heat, and settled into a slow, lazy slog, Lucy took out her umbrella and reopened it.

"Well, Mary Poppins, if we get lost, I guess you'll fly us home," Freddy said, proud of himself for what Lucy deemed a stupid comment and dismissed it.

They trucked along, their mood was vibrant with thoughts of cool spring water to drink and swim in, yet with each notch of the sun ratcheting itself into hotter temperatures, their excitement receded into silence. For once they didn't talk, eyes turned toward the distant dark woods, thick with mealy pines, briars, and bramble.

Chapter
9

The Jungle

The main road went from shells and pebbles to only a hint of a road. Speckled with trampled and upright weeds, it ran into the woods and disappeared. They stopped to take in their surroundings at the edge of the jungle, and Lucy closed her umbrella, tucking it into her daypack. Freddy took out his guidebook and flipped through the pages. The book was thin and worn with a map of the island.

Moving under a jacaranda tree for shade, Freddy said, "Here it is, Squash Beach. The instructions suggest trekkers go straight from the road into the woods until they come to a rock that looks like a ball. At the ball take a right. Then at the shale overhanging, go left into the pine forest. The floor of the pine forest should be filled with copper-colored needles. If not, *you bumbling fools entered the wrong forest.* If the correct forest, walk through it. Once at the top, rest and take in the view, unless there are too many trees. At the dead oak tree, go straight down until you reach the ocean. If lucky, you've arrived at

Squash Beach." Freddy looked up at Lucy. "I wonder if the guy who wrote this was drunk?"

Lucy asked to see the book. She glanced over the directions, then flipped to the copyright page. "This was written in 1982; it's ten years old." She made a resigning *humph* noise.

"It was cheap. Besides, I bet the ball rock is still there." Freddy flipped through to the map and showed Lucy the plump crescent-shaped island and said, "The map couldn't have changed."

"Were there any restaurants then?" Leaning into each other, they skimmed over the lodging and eating section. It was very basic such as, "One should bring camping equipment: stove, pots, fork, knife, and a fishing rod, although supporting the local fishermen would be nice. People will also invite you in for a meal, the price? Reasonable. And if you don't want to camp, pay someone to stay in their house, although you will be kicking someone out of their bed."

"I would have liked to have been on the island in 1982. Stone Age stuff," Freddy commented.

"I like the way it is now…I like my room. And I like restaurants."

"I know what you mean. Well, off to find the ball." Freddy shut the guidebook and tucked it into a pocket of his daypack by an orange. He then made a royal bow and waved his hand to prompt Lucy to go first.

As they stepped into the thicket of trees that had a woven, almost hermetically sealed canopy above them, the rays of the sun immediately vanished, and the atmosphere turned musty and dark. The humidity thickened and they both groaned. Not a wag of wind; the mosquitoes whizzed around like an old-fashioned battle charge and attacked with brutal precision. The hungry blood-sucking pests clipped their ears and pinched their calves. A slapping frenzy prevailed, then stopped. Reaching into her day pack, Lucy took out some sort of DEET mixture she had bought in Copan and profusely sprayed Freddy and herself. It smelled like butterscotch, which made them mumble something about wanting candy. Resuming their trek, they talked about Halloween and bite-size pieces of chocolates, caramel twists, and candy corn. In the stray beams of light, swarms of small gnats resembled clouds of dust. Having spent the past few weeks in the sun and sand, the new terrain drew them in with interest, awe, and horror. The earth was littered with giant curled-up leaves, logs, sticks, and flowers that glowed bluish, purple, white, and pink. Butterflies bounced in and out of the flowers and briars, while rich sod sunk beneath their feet.

As they walked, the idea of eating candy dissipated and turned to inexhaustible comments about the different shades of bark, the speed of hummingbirds, the weird warble of a grackle's croak, and the creepy sound of grebe's bleating whoop, and so on and so forth. The uneven ground and mud caused them to waddle at times, as their sneakers were sucked into the goo. When the land made an uptick and the soupy dirt disappeared, life became less cumbersome. Especially after kicking the crud off their shoes. They also took a few minutes to stand still and comment on the heat and sticky cobwebs.

"This is hideous," Freddy said, pulling dead bugs off his face.

"I don't recall Robinson Crusoe having issues with spiders," Lucy remarked.

"I don't recall bugs on that island."

They were both unwilling to retreat since the beach could be just around a tree trunk, even if the guidebook said otherwise.

Continuing, they finally came across a rock that was perfectly round. "The ball rock!" they shouted in unison while jumping for joy.

Following the directions, they went right but not too far right because that would send them away from the hill and not up it. Lucy remembered she had a compass, dug into her day pack, and pulled out the jack-in-the-box prize. "I think we need to keep east but not too far east or we'll go backward," she commented.

"Where did you get that?"

"It was a prize." Lucy's face was flushed, and she pushed back wisps of brown hair that were matted to her forehead and neck. "How long do you think we have been walking?"

"Hard to tell." Freddy's shirt was drenched and darkened by sweat; he pulled it up to wipe his face. Lucy noticed his hairy stomach was shiny. It caused her to think about hair, and she was happy not to have hair on her stomach because the hair on her head made her hot enough.

Standing in silence, the unspoken thought of turning back finally rattled their determination. But it was a fleeting thought of silence between the two of them and vanished with the idea of swimming in the ocean. "I can't wait to swim," Freddy beamed.

"I can't either."

"Do you think a step is a minute?" Freddy inquired.

"Could be."

"Let's count our steps to the top. We can see how long it takes us."

Counting their steps was tedious. They stopped at number twenty-two.

"Look at that, a snake." Freddy pointed with his eyes at a long, winding creature slithering along the ground. He took his hat off and fanned himself while inching backward. Lucy stopped too. She took a few steps toward Freddy to get a better look. The snake wended away from them, effortlessly over fallen green tuber-shaped leaves. The sound was of crinkling paper. "Five feet," Lucy mumbled in a low voice.

"Or longer," Freddy whispered, frozen in place, his hands visibly shaking. He ogled the snake as it disappeared into a hole, then he made a groaning whimper. Placing his hand over his heart, he said, "I don't like snakes. I think they might be in my shoes before putting them on or in the cupboard in my room where I put my clothes."

"Possibly a fer-de-lance." Lucy's voice hinted at intrigue, and she glanced at Freddy to see his expression, his fear a juggernaut to toy with. And although Lucy wasn't sure what a fer-de-lance looked like, it was the only horribly acting snake she knew about in the area. "They're deadly."

"I've read about them." Freddy's eyes grew wide. He stepped farther back from where the assumed grim reaper had been.

"I'll protect you." She picked up a club-like stick. It was as thick as a leg and had a knotty fist at one end. "We should walk single file."

"That's nice of you." He gave her an odd look, as though something had become inverted, and he wasn't sure if he liked it; yet overall, for the time being, he was fine with Lucy and her club taking the lead.

They once again resumed their walk. This time they kept their sights focused on the ground in front of them with an eye on the periphery. They kept quiet too, hoping the snake wouldn't detect them. But when a red dwarf squirrel ran behind Freddy, it caused him to twist around and yelp, and Lucy laughed. Freddy wasn't amused and told her so, but once a discussion about the beauty of a red coat versus a gray coat on an animal came into play, he forgot about being miffed. However, the conversation didn't change the fact that there might be dangerous snakes around, but it took away the seriousness of it, and Freddy announced that he would now take the lead. "It's the manly thing to do," Freddy muttered. Lucy thought if that was how Freddy wanted to think, it was fine by her, but she kept her club in case they were attacked from behind. "I heard red squirrels like to bite redheads." She giggled.

When a shale overhang appeared by thorny bushes with magenta-colored flowers, they made little jumps of joy. To the left, just like the guidebook said, was the pristine flooring of copper-colored needles and hundreds of the pine trees that created it. This forest lacked webbing and vines as though it had been cleared. Freddy and Lucy were under the impression fairies might pop out from behind the trees. The light filtering through the evergreens resembled flashlights from above. "Neverland," Lucy said in a wondrous tone. Freddy began to sing, "I won't grow up, I don't..." Lucy joined in, laughing.

They marched forward in this manner for several feet, singing all the lyrics, then stopped, out of breath and dripping with sweat. Lucy took a sip of her water. It was less than half full. "Not much left." She glanced at Freddy, who was gulping large chugs until his plastic bottle crackled and folded in.

"Well, I'm out," he said as water dripped from his chin. Then he added, "Don't drink anymore; we need to ration yours."

"Doesn't seem right."

"We have oranges. And when we find the spring...lots of fresh water."

"I suppose."

They took up the trek again with languid steps, Freddy whistling and Lucy humming the *Peter Pan* tune. Once out of the pine forest and into a small savanna, the trees that surrounded the opening were short and sparse. "I think we're at the top," Lucy surmised. It lacked a view of any type, but then the guidebook said it might not have one. Sitting down on a large, craggy rock, they read that the lost spring bubbled up from under a layer of hardened lava somewhere along the one-mile stretch of beach. Hungry, they ate one of the oranges. When a bird nearby made a sound like clicking castanets and several more followed, Freddy made a *O* with his mouth and said, "My God, vultures already."

"Quails," Lucy replied. "Is that the oak tree?" She was pointing at a rotted stump with a large crumbled trunk lying next to it.

"Listen," Freddy said, his index finger to his lips. They both sat barely breathing, intent on hearing something. A distant muffled roar of waves crashing could be heard. "It's right below us." They walked over to a patch of russet-colored bushes and peered over them. The beach looked like one big gray rock that went on for miles, and the dark aqua-blue waters pounded at the volcanic barrier. The reverie of the sea and the cawing twill of birds and the beauty below filled them with excitement and a sense of awe.

Freddy fanned himself with his hat, his usually wavy, thick, brassy hair lay flat and matted. "Gosh, I hope we find the spring. I could use a sip of Mother Earth's sweet water."

Lucy watched Freddy put the lip of her bottle of water to his mouth, and he took a measured sip. She wanted to ask him if he had brushed his teeth but thought not. Since she had gotten to know him better, she figured he might feel slighted. She took the plastic bottle back, secretly wiped the opening, and drank tentatively. She then screwed the top back on and said, "No more. This water is for the walk back."

Chapter
10

The Detective

Liam awoke slowly, beginning with a moan, along with a rub to his mouth and forehead. The sound of the tide brushed against the unkempt water line; rocks, bramble, seaweed, and the occasional candy wrapper and bottle cap bewildered him. When birds squawked and chirped, he opened his eyes and realized where he was. "Oh, the island. What a shame." He had no idea how long he had been asleep. His body felt crusty, and the intense sun on his arms and face gave him the feeling of being cooked alive.

His back damp from the dewy ground and sweat, he looked at his hands, red and hot to the touch. He poked his skin to make sure it wasn't just his imagination; when white spots appeared, he grumbled, "Burnt, fuck." He shook his head with disbelief, then quickly stopped due to the excruciating pain it caused his brain. Thirsty, he crawled onto his knees and haunches, and then using the help of the thin branches of a natty bush, he righted himself. "Now, where is that bottle of booze?" A waft of body odor came along with the low tide, and he paused to sniff himself. He concluded he stunk, but so did the island.

He recalled the only other time he had fallen so far into a mire of intoxication. It occurred after his child was born. He went on a bender in the township where his mistress lived, although she wasn't his mistress yet. Still in love with his wife, having sex with another wasn't on his mind, although drinking heavily was. House and bar hopping, Liam ended up asleep with the garbage and rats at the backside of a makeshift restaurant. The woman he would eventually bed and call his mistress rescued him from being eaten alive by mad dogs. *Never again*, he had said to himself, but here he was, no doubt resembling a first-rate down-on-his-luck wino. Calling himself to attention, he castigated, "You are to quit tomorrow. As for today? Let's celebrate quitting." He eyed his whiskey bottle on the ground and picked it up to empty the last few drops onto his tongue. The harsh liquid seared his parched throat. He coughed, reached into his pants pocket for a crumbled pack of cigarettes, and lit one of the crooked smokes. He then coughed, hacked up phlegm, and spat, "Why, I'm a model of health," and spat again.

He saw the mail boat hadn't left yet. Still docked, it listed gently back and forth and appeared vacant. The trip over to the island fuzzy and filled with snippets of chatting with the crew, he remembered a pretty girl, fresh-looking with a nice body, and a chubby older man who pinched his bottom. "Fresh coot," he mumbled. He then panicked and darted his eyes around the ground. With a smile, he realized his attaché was slung over his shoulder. His mind foggy but churning, he began to recall more of the boat ride. "That's right," he muttered. "The girl knows something. Those exquisite green eyes of hers widened when she heard his name."

Trying to think which name lit her eyes up more, Heraldo or Harry, he gave up because it strained his head too much. However, he did conclude that even when drunk, he was a splendid detective. *I will need to check again with that wayward crew. Re-show them the pictures and apply pressure to tell the truth. I could threaten to have them fired, or better yet, thrown in jail for aiding and abetting a fugitive.* The taste of impending success aroused a need to find more whiskey. He looked around for a store or even better, a bar. The first thing he saw was the sign *Juanita's Tienda* at the top of the knoll and began the slow slog up the ascent. Unable to deal with his duffel, he left it behind to be retrieved later.

"Good morning," Fabio said to Liam.

Liam looked at the bird, perplexed. He then wiped the sweat from his brow, tossed his spent cigarette to the ground, and glanced around to see if somebody else had spoken. Since there was only the bird, he replied, "Well, good morning to you too."

"What a great day to be in love," Fabio spoke, then sang. "Freddddy...Freddddy."

Puzzled by such a gregarious creature since he had never met a talkative bird before, it caused him to wonder if he might be hallucinating due to what had become an almost two-week bender. He let a few moments of silence pass. Then, with a corner of his mouth curled, he decided he was sober, which caused the need for liquor to become even more urgent.

"Freddy," the bird said again, which stopped Liam from walking away.

Liam recalled a case in Johannesburg in which a parrot cracked a murder case due to exposing the criminal. *Possibly this bird knows a thing or two.* "Do you know a fellow named Heraldo? Or what is his other name? Harry."

Fabio cocked his head and said, "No."

This caused Liam to laugh. "I'll pluck you naked if you don't tell me the truth."

"Hey mister, I *don'* like people threatening my bird." Arnoldo stood in the doorway wagging his index finger. He had a scowl plastered across his face.

Liam caught the disdain and replied, "Just having fun." He then picked at his fingernails and sighed. "Say, you don't happen to sell whiskey."

"Sure, mon."

"I'd love a bottle. The best you have."

"Wait here. Yah, don' smell so great." Arnoldo walked back into the store.

Liam sniffed his armpits for the second time. The odor reminded him of a peeled onion. *A shower would be luxurious*, he thought. Then another idea darted in. He dug into his pants pocket for the key to his attaché; he wanted to show the bird and the surly store owner the pictures of the criminals he was after. But all he found was money, a soggy mint, and a packet of crumbled cigarettes. He lit one. He glanced down to the water's edge at his duffel and took a large drag, then exhaled the blue smoke out his nose. Liam assumed the key had fallen out and was somewhere in the dirt. Too lazy to go fetch it, he sighed and wished there was a seat for him to sit down on. He looked around and saw a tiny stool by the door. He ambled his way over and sat. From his seat, Liam, with his cigarette hung from the side of his mouth, playfully squawked like a parrot at Fabio. He liked the sound so much, he did it several more times.

Fabio replied, "Eleanor loves mail."

"Eleanor. Right, that's her name. Why thank you, bird." He chuckled. He then thought to squawk again, but it had hurt his throat, so instead, he spoke, "Fuck, you're fun. Now what about Harry? Do you know him?"

Arnoldo came out of the store. "You interrogating my bird again?"

"No. We're merely having a conversation."

Arnoldo did not respond. Instead, he sucked on his teeth and squinched his face, skeptical of Liam's intentions. He had a bottle of Wild Turkey in his hands and walked over to him, "Twenty Limps."

Arnoldo's pudgy pecker smiled at Liam, curled into a crescent, like a giant pistachio. Liam thought of eating peanuts, then shook his head to counter such a notion and shifted his focus to Arnoldo's face; he was grinning as though he had won something. Liam clicked his teeth as though finding being sober disturbing, and pulled a couple of crumpled lempiras out of his pants' pocket and paid him. Arnoldo gave him the whiskey, along with a sugar banana. "For Fabio, not you." And went back into the store.

He held both items in his hands, got up, and walked over to Fabio. "Your owner is strange," he said and blew smoke into the cage. Fabio stepped away.

"Let's try a little bribery." But before he started his questioning, Liam cracked open the whiskey bottle and took a long, soothing draw. He then held the sugar banana in front of the cage and said, "Harry and Eleanor."

Fabio cocked his head and eyed the sugar banana but said nothing. Liam repeated the names several times. When he unpeeled the banana to possibly make it more enticing, Fabio sang, "Harry and Eleanor sitting in a tree."

Liam laughed. "This is all so nuts. What else can you tell me?" And he fed Fabio the banana. The bird munched it down his gullet, and Fabio immediately turned his back to Liam. He was done.

Liam took another swig and burped. "Hold on now. We're not through."

Fabio refused to look at him.

"Damn, I should have held off feeding you. Well, we'll try this again later."

Letting out another belch and feeling the acid in his stomach clench his chest and stab his belly, he realized he needed food. He thought about the store but then spotted Milly's Gin & Cerveza and went over. A chalkboard stuck in the gravel announced today's special, "Grouper Tacos." He sat down at the counter. No one was around. So, he got up and went to the back of the restaurant. An old refrigerator, a broken metal shelf, and a couple of plastic chairs were by a crumbled stone wall. Beyond the wall, a broad savanna went all the way to the leeward side of the island to the ocean. The ocean went all the way to the horizon. Liam stood for a moment to take in the beauty of the sun and the wheat-colored earth. Then moody thoughts of responsibility brought him back to reality. He muttered, "I could live in paradise if it weren't for my parents and their stingy ways."

The faint cataract of laughter interrupted his inner diatribe toward his family. Shifting his stance, he peered over to the back of the store. Four people were huddled around a table. They were looking at a large piece of paper. By their feet, chickens milled around and pecked at the ground.

"Yoo-hoo," he said and waved his arm over his head. All four glanced at him. Liam recognized Eleanor, Arnoldo, the old man, Juan, but not the curvy woman wearing a colorful head scarf.

"Hallo. Is anyone serving food?" he shouted.

The curvy woman replied, "*Naw*, not yet. Go to the No Name past the Beach Lodge."

Liam frowned. He was too hungry and pooped to make that trek without food. Not sure what to do, he watched Eleanor lean into Juan and say something. Juan then leaned into Arnoldo, who leaned over the table to talk to the curvy woman. They then stopped what they were doing to stare back at Liam like cows in a pasture. Liam stared back at them. They appeared to be talking to each other while eyeing him suspiciously. It was obvious they were chatting about him. He smacked his lips and let out a clump of stuck air that had phlegm in it and spat. "Right," Liam finally replied. "I'll just get a move on." He took a swig from his bottle and went to walk away, then thought better of it. He felt they weren't treating him fairly, and it was mean to talk about a person in front of them. He was miffed, and his mind stormed him into an angry box. He turned back around and burst, "You're all suspects!" Their eyes pinned on him like little needles. His mouth pursed, and he nodded accusingly at the little group, who went back to ignoring him.

"I have questions for you. I know you know stuff. Criminals! All of you!"

All four took a deep breath, shoulders lifted, then relaxed, but no one bothered to look at him again. It seemed the large sheet of paper on the table was much more interesting.

Liam shrugged. Furious at his lack of discipline and impulsiveness, he scolded himself for being too overt and possibly ruining the advent of surprise. He downed an enormous swig of whiskey and lit another cigarette on top of the one he already had in his hand but had forgotten about. When he walked by the food "specials" sign, he kicked it, knocking it over. Grumbly, he felt tomorrow would be apprised of a better opportunity to ask them all about the "Harry" fellow, and maybe after a bath, they wouldn't recognize him. To start anew. With great bitterness, he concluded he could use a nap. Since he preferred a bed over the soggy, rocky ground, he decided to seek out the Beach Lodge. Besides, he had read it was the only place to stay.

He walked back down to the bay's edge to collect his duffel. He couldn't help but think there was something else he needed. "The lost key?" He looked for something shiny, but the only bright objects were bottle tops. He stared at the long dock and the mail boat and took a draw from his bottle, and a drag off his newly lit cig while he tossed the other burnt-out one away. The whiskey was tangy in his mouth; he tugged again on his cigarette and exhaled. *Could I have left the key on the boat?* The booze and lack of food caused him to hiccup, while his mind struggled to think. Better to nap and get the key tomorrow. Then he smiled at his attaché that was limp by his side. "Why, I'll bash you open," he said and set off toward the Beach Lodge. His duffel slung over his shoulder caused him to grunt periodically. When he walked past the church, he paused to rest and to observe the children who sat at their desks, while a skinny teacher lectured them. One little girl had a donkey standing beside her. "I would have loved to have brought the family donkey to school," he mumbled and set off again. He weaved and stumbled his way down the road.

When he finally arrived at the Beach Lodge, Ernesto, the innkeeper, was out front. He sat in a plastic chair. His large belly was pushed tight against the arms and the plastic legs were strained. On his lap, he had a colorful ceramic plate full of french fries and a dollop of ketchup. He ate one fry at a time with his pinky out, dipping each fry with grace. The top of his bald head was sweaty, along with his upper lip.

Since he had his bag of keys on him, he handed one to Liam, and Liam gave him a clump of money, including a soggy mint.

"The room is on the second floor with a view of the street. The ocean views are taken," Ernest lied. The room was hot and ugly, and he hoped it would discourage the man from staying long. Ernesto didn't like heavy day drinkers, himself an exception. It was only midmorning and a cooler filled with beer was by his foot, another opened by the chair. Ernesto suggested he should take a shower or go for a swim before touching the bed. "You won't get your deposit back if you ruin the room."

"Now, you're the third person to mention my scent. Me being one of them." Liam raised an eyebrow and asked, "Can I swim naked?"

"Why don't you swim in your clothes." Ernesto, more interested in his fries than talking to Liam, began eating again.

There was a wire rack with various bags of chips leaning against the wall by Ernesto. Liam bought three beers, a bottle of water, and four bags of chips. He then made his way through the lower hallway; his duffel scraped the floor and left bits of dirt behind. He put everything by the door to the beach, except for his attaché and whiskey bottle. Stumbling over the sand, he made his way to the ocean. He ignored Ernesto's suggestion of swimming in his clothes because he desired the freedom of being naked. Liam stripped and left his attaché by his haphazardly tossed clothes before entering the water. With his bottle of whiskey, he waded in, fell backward into the ocean, and swam around like an otter: bottle on his chest, head tilted up, his feet peddling whimsically.

Chapter
11

Squash Beach

The scruffy terrain of the hillside was speckled with windswept trees. To glance over the edge was harrowing and caused Lucy and Freddy to have a touch of vertigo. They pushed aside thoughts of falling and shuffled their way down. The raucous roar of the sea and constant wind excited and unsettled them at the same time. Not another soul around, they felt like the only two people in the universe on the verge of discovering the elixir to longevity, water. It made them giddy, where the challenging terrain made them miserable. For the most part, the path down the hill was steep and filled with loose rocks and cacti. It caused their footing to be unreliable, and they slipped a lot. Grunting, they also cursed: "Shit," and "Fuck that bush. Why are we fucking doing this?" and "Whose stupid idea was this? Shit! Fuck!"

When the descent flattened, they stopped and looked tentatively at each other. Feeling that a certain danger had just passed, they were elated to stand on level ground. Lucy could hear her heartbeat and saw that Freddy was out of breath. "No wonder the spring is lost," she said.

Freddy laughed. Lucy laughed too. It felt good to laugh.

They made their way through the eclectic foliage to the beach, cedars, pines, and fruit trees; a banana and a pineapple tree caught Lucy's attention. She checked both for ripe fruit, but none had any. As they stepped out onto the beach. too windy for her umbrella, she took out suntan lotion and lathered it all over her face, then treaded her eyes over the ocean, the sky, and the beach and said, "It's perfect here."

"Lovely," Freddy said, breathing in big gulps of the air through his nose. When his hat blew off, he snapped forward and caught it before it flew out of reach.

As far as they could see, the beach was nothing but melded lava rocks with dips and pointy upturns. The porous surface looked as though someone had taken spiky shoes and walked all over it. Down the beach, the ocean hit the rocks with such velocity that the scene resembled a spluttering geyser. Where they stood was mellower, but the waters were still mighty. They could feel its pull.

"Not swimmable," Freddy mumbled.

Lucy spotted a stumpy palm tree and burst, "Look, coconuts. I love coconut juice." They broke two off and immediately tried to break them open. They bashed the coconuts on the knife-like rocks, but the coconuts just bounced back at them. They threw them up against trees, but they just ricocheted into the woods. Frustrated, they stopped.

"What's that?" Freddy pointed at an enclosed pool of water by the ocean's edge.

The size of two large Jacuzzis, the pool was protected by a ledge.

When a wave came in, the water rose but not by much. When the wave receded, it was only by a small amount. The pool was clear like glass, and the bottom, layered with white coral sand. They had bathing suits underneath their clothing and stripped. Dipping their bodies into the water, they dunked their overheated heads repeatedly. Lucy then stood with her feet flat on the sandy bottom. The water was deep enough to cover her shoulders, and she began to scoop out bits of dirt and bramble they had added. Freddy sat on a rock low in the water and began to toss the debris out, too. Lucy also found a submerged rock high and sat. The pool was wonderful, and they kept looking at each other and smiling.

They felt rejuvenated and justly rewarded for their buggy and hot trek. Hungry, they ate all four bags of chips and split the last orange. Freddy suggested trying to open the coconuts again because he was thirsty and they needed the last of their water for the walk home. When he got out, his big body waterlogged, he dripped and dripped, so he shook himself like a dog. Lucy did the same, and it made them both laugh. They put their sneakers back on to prevent scraping up their feet on the lava.

"We need a machete," Lucy said and banged her coconut against the ground, then watched it fly into the air and land several yards away, while Freddy's coconut went into the ocean.

"I'd like to swim again," Freddy said.

They got back into the pool and sat on their rock seats. They blew bubbles in the water with their mouths, and when bubble blowing wasn't fun anymore, they laid their heads back and stared at the sky. "I could sleep here," Lucy murmured. She flicked her umbrella open. Resting her head against the pool's edge, she placed it over her face to sleep. But the air became too hot, and she shut it and swam around in little circles. When she looked over at Freddy, she saw him trying to fight off sleep. His head against the rocks, his eyes were shut, then opened, then shut again for good. His *O* mouth began hissing a fluted tune like a warthog rooting with a whistle. Lucy thought that Lyla had to be a very patient person to sleep with that sound.

She then looked out over the ocean. Amused by the grebes diving in and out of the water, she loved to see them grab small fish and eat them while flying. The sun, the foam on the waves, and the deep blue water melted Lucy's thoughts into somnolent tranquility. Then something pinched her toe. She jerked and jumped out to sit on the periphery. Once the pool water calmed down, she saw a salmon-colored crab walking along the pool floor. It reached for the sky with claws twice its size. She decided it would be best to stay out and look for the spring.

Chapter
12

The Missing Folder

It was late afternoon when Liam awoke from his nap. Only wearing a pair of boxers, he lay flat on the twin-size bed. His head felt heavy on the thin pillow, and his legs were falling off the sides. Staring at the ceiling in a stupor, he let out a long *ahhhh*, then grimaced at the foul taste in his mouth and took a small sip from the whiskey bottle next to him, swished, and swallowed. Eyeing the piddly remains in the bottle, he muttered something about gnomes drinking his liquor while he slept. Sitting up, he couldn't quite recall why he was in such a shabby, pointless-looking room. Spotting his attaché by the door, he said, "That's right. I must find the criminals." He was amazed at his good memory since he spent so much time trying to ruin it. He readjusted his member, then rose and walked over to his attaché. He picked it up and cursed. He didn't have the key.

Moving over to the window, he stood scouting the road below for something hard. Across the street were several large rocks. Smiling, he lifted his briefcase into the air, and with an overhanded thrust, he threw it out the window. It hit the rocks and popped open. Jubilant, he gave a little jump of joy, then frowned. His passport, American Express checks, and a clump of what he considered useless cash (lempiras) were splattered all over the street. Fearful an islander or a thieving tourist might steal it, he ran out of the room, down the steps, through the open front door, and by Ernesto who was still in his plastic chair. A pile of empty dirty plates by his feet, he was sound asleep, snoring.

Liam gathered up his stuff and the broken case and went back up to his room. Sitting cross-legged on the bed, he glanced over the contents. An ugly feeling gripped his stomach. Where was the folder? He ran back down the steps and over to the rocks again. He checked the crevasses; he looked under the nearby bushes, leaves, and twisted flower heads. But it wasn't there. Panicked, he ran back up to his room, taking two steps at a time. Once back in the room, he began to pace back and forth. *Think, Liam, think. Where could that folder have gone to?* Struck by an aha moment, he quickly dressed, grabbing anything wearable from his duffel, Jams with seals, and an okra button-down shirt. Exhausted by his frenzied activity, he drank a bottle of water, then grabbed his whiskey, gulped down the remains, and left.

Storming by Ernesto, he tripped on the pile of dirty plates and fell knees first onto the dirt road. "Fat pig!" he shouted at the snoozing man, along with wailing over the pain. Having scraped his knees, he licked the small trickles of blood with his tongue and then dabbed the cuts with his shirt. "Fuck, I can't wait to leave this disgusting place." Getting back up on his feet, he walked with long, brisk strides to the dock, hoping the mail boat was still there. Head full of steam, his mind stewed with violent thoughts: *The bitch took it. Trying to save Heraldo, are you? Well, not so fast.* If she didn't talk, he would bash her face into putty, then throw her into one of Honduras's putrid jails. He then stopped for a moment to hold his aching head in hands. *I could use some aspirin,* he moaned.

He dashed into Juanita's Tienda and bought some aspirin, along with a can of Coca-Cola to wash the pills down with. Juanita happened to be behind the counter with Bob. Liam stood in front of the two, drinking and burping. The bubbles in the Coke were helping settle his stomach. He then thought to try his luck with a few questions regarding his case. "Do you know a fellow named Heraldo? He may be going by the name Harry?"

Juanita said, "No."

Liam looked at the donkey as though he would answer, too, then laughed. "What am I thinking?" Then to Juanita, "That bird of yours sure has a mouth. Do you have any sugar bananas? I may try bribing him again." But then he remembered something more crucial. "Never mind. Is the mail boat still here?"

Juanita waved her hand in front of her nose. "Would you like to buy some mints?"

"My breath that bad? Okay, a pack of Juicy Fruit and the cigs in the brown box."

"The mail boat is still here," she said while tallying up the goods. The news planted him in a rush. Liam paid scattering change on the counter in his frenzy to leave. Then as though he were the wind, the door slammed shut behind him, and Juanita was left with an essence of stale, boozy breath.

He peered down at the dock and saw the boat, lit a cigarette, and exhaled a billowy cloud of smoke. *I think I'll greet you with a great big slap.* He then growled, "I hate fucking bitches. My wife is one," and ran down the hill. When he came to the dock, he slowed himself to a trot, and then stopped to think about what it was he was doing, *Oh, that's right, thieves. I need to catch the thieves.*

Once at the mail boat, he paused to assess the situation because no one seemed to be around. "Halloo," he said, then remained silent to listen for voices. But all he heard was the light lapping of water against the boat and the fluttering pages of a book by the cooler. Then from somewhere came an echo of laughter. He looked behind him, down the dock, then over the bay. There was a trawler with three people in it nearly fifty yards away. He shouted, "Yoo-hoo!" When no one turned his way, he shouted again and waved his arm over his head. The small group turned around and looked at him.

He recognized the mail crew, Juan and Eleanor. Arnoldo was standing next to Juan. "I need to speak to you people. A police matter! Come here!" Liam shouted.

They ignored him. They had fishing lines in the water, and they began reeling them in and recasting.

"I won't be ignored!" he shouted. "All of you, arrested, unless you come here immediately!"

They continued to ignore him. Frustrated, Liam jumped into the boat and went into the pilothouse. He wanted to turn the engine on and go over and get them. While he was staring at all the nobs and not finding a key to start the engine in any of the drawers, he realized his plan seemed futile, so he walked back onto the deck. He gazed over at the three who were fishing and shouted, "You can't stay out there forever!" then belched a waft of boozy bile. Rubbing his stomach, he unraveled a piece of Juicy Fruit, popped it into his mouth, and lit a cigarette. Chewing and smoking, he remained staring for a few minutes at what he considered to be three errant fugitives. Since none of them would look at him again, he went over to the cooler and took a beer, cracked it open, and drank all of it in one draft. Cold, it relaxed his fervent temper but only temporarily. The sun beating like fire upon his head made him hot and foggy. He thought to jump in the water and swim over. *The coolness would be delightful*, but then thought not. *Once*

I got to the boat, they would most likely hit me with something, and I would drown. Irritated and growing morose over having to drink beer when what he really wanted was whiskey, he shouted, "It's a small island. I'll get you later!" He then scolded himself for letting them know his plans. "Oh, bugger me stupid," he mumbled to himself and scrambled out of the boat. As he walked down the dock, he mumbled, "The obstinateness of lowlifes. Pathetic wastes of my time," and "The law's on my side, not yours...hahaha."

At the main road, Liam walked aimlessly back toward the Beach Lodge. When he approached the colorful row houses, he spotted a man with eyes that looked like fried eggs. He was drinking a beer and leaning out a glassless window staring at the road. Liam stopped, "Say, my good man. Do you have another beer or, better yet, some whiskey?"

The man waved him in. The place was dark and smelled like fish and grease. Florence was frying a barracuda that the man had caught early in the day. Three local men were sitting playing dominoes at the kitchen table waiting to eat. The man with the egg eyes gave Liam a beer and brought over another chair for him. He wanted to pay, but the man said no. "But if he wanted whiskey, it was forty *'limps'* for a bottle." Liam thought to protest the price, but then if they kicked him out, he would have to walk all the way to the store to get another. He paid for the whiskey and joined the game, concluding that he had done enough detective work for one day.

Chapter
13

A Better Path

Lucy wandered down the beach. She poked at seaweed and pushed twigs and other natural refuse with her foot. The guidebook had said the spring was hidden. Hidden in what manner, she wasn't sure. She looked at the woods and saw a frumpy banana plant and went over to it. Their lunch was more of a snack, and she was still hungry. A ripe sweet banana would be satisfying and pleasant to eat, she had thought. The cluster of bananas was dark green and not edible. She then noticed a couple of withered cypress trees, which folded around an opening into the dark forest. She went over and saw it was a path. She followed the path with her eyes, and it appeared to broaden and turn into a soggy dirt road. There were several tire treads indented in the mud, and the road seemed to go on forever.

Entering, she followed the road until she saw it went around the hill they had just climbed and descended. The deep rutted tire marks, small and large, grew thicker, and in places, it looked like someone may have gotten stuck. The idea that people had driven out to the beach was disappointing. She had it in her head that the beach and their little pool were secluded, hidden from the others and that no one ever went to this part of the island. But now she knew that wasn't true. She walked back out of the woods and looked for Freddy to tell him the disheartening news. He was still by their swimming pool but had gotten out. He stood a few feet away from it with a stick in his hands that looked like a divining rod. It appeared he couldn't decide which end went toward the ground and which end he should hold.

"Freddy!" she shouted and waved her arm over her head at him.

He looked around but didn't see her and went back to his stick. Holding the fork end, the long end was on the ground, and he began being led in circles.

"Freddy," Lucy said again. Having made her way down the rocks, she walked up to him and tapped his shoulder. She'd never touched Freddy before and found his hefty shoulder damp, and it felt foreign and...not quite right. "Freddy," she said again keeping her hands to her side.

"What?" He whirled around and almost knocked her over.

"I found a road." Then she looked at his stick and added, "You've got a divining rod."

"A what?"

"We call it a divining rod," she said.

"Yes. I only found one. You should look for one too. Now, what do you mean about a road?"

"Follow me."

He put his stick down, and the two of them went over to the woods by the cypress trees. Lucy brought her daypack with her and took out her compass. "I believe it curves around the hill but stays near the ocean. If we took this route back, we'll probably end up...let's look at the map again."

Freddy retrieved his daypack in order to get the guidebook. Huddling together, they flipped through the pages to the map and studied it. "We could have skipped the hill," Lucy said. "I believe the road goes to the dive shop."

Freddy bit his lower lip. "I don't like that a road comes here. It depresses me. I thought the place was ours," then added, "Where did you learn to read a compass?"

"I was a Girl Scout."

"I've seen American movies with Girl Scouts. They're mean."

"Do you think I'm mean?"

"Sometimes. I haven't won a bet yet." Freddy puffed his cheeks and narrowed his eyes.

Lucy shook her head, then smiled. "I have a bet. I bet this road leads us to the dive shop." She held out her hand to shake on it.

"That's not fair. I was going to say that," Freddy huffed.

"Think of another bet then."

"I bet. I bet...we don't see a giraffe on the way back."

Lucy laughed. "You're being silly now. No, I take that back. You're being a big baby. There aren't any giraffes on the island."

"My bet."

Not wanting to appear mean, she said, "Okay, a pilito." Then she added, unable to help herself, "I think you have issues."

"Yes, I most likely do. But then who doesn't?"

She wanted to say some people have bigger issues than others but didn't want to open a can of worms for Freddy to elaborate either on his or her issues. So, she just shook his hand.

Freddy looked up at the sky. According to the sun, it was near sunset. "Where does all the time go?" Freddy mused as they walked into the woods and onto the muddy road. The musty smell, the darkness, the mysterious aura of making their way into the unknown, silenced them. When a flurry of gnats swarmed their faces, they stopped to apply bug spray, then continued on. They saw a toucan and a small mouse; several spiderwebs and red squirrels; and heard the crinkling of leaves, which they assumed to be fer-de-lances. As there were no giraffes, Lucy handed Freddy a pilito when they stepped out of the woods onto a shallow ledge overlooking the dive shop. Glancing across the ocean at the sky, the only remnants of the sun were the pinks and streaks of white at the horizon. The ocean was much calmer than Squash Beach. It licked gently at the sandy, rocky shore.

They stood by a cluster of red heliconia flowers and glanced over the dive compound. The only other gas pump on the island sat at the end of the shop's dock, a rusted round upright rectangle with bold letters that said, *GAS*. Although Arnoldo insisted it didn't work, it did. Lucy knew this because she had helped Josey pump gas into his dirt bike and boat. A few yards away from the tank, a twenty-eight-foot Parker mildly swayed against the dock. It was Josey's dive boat. The whole place seemed abandoned the way sunsets have a way of making the earth look tucked in and ready for bed.

Lucy wondered if Josey had returned and was possibly in the main building located at the end of the dock. Grabbing hold of Freddy's shirt, she went to drag him over to a window by the door. Skidding backward at first, he eventually complied but only after pulling her hand away. "I don't like being dragged around."

"It's a habit. I don't know why I do it. Don't be angry."

"I'm not angry. But you do it a lot."

"Fine, I won't do it again," Lucy said.

"I bet you will."

They shook hands.

Peering into the window of the shop, they saw Mateo writing nitrogen-oxygen ratios on a blackboard. His dreadlocks were piled into a beehive on top of his head. He was shirtless, and his wiry, muscled arms pulsed as he wrote. He had a cropped Fu Manchu mustache and beard that he methodically tugged on whenever he stopped to think. Lucy knew that Mateo, like Josey, often slept with the female tourists. But where Josey didn't seem to have a type, Mateo favored shapely blondes with ruby-red lipstick, and itsy-bitsy bikinis. It made Josey laugh and say, "When girls find this out, if they didn't come here blonde, they somehow become blonde." Dive equipment was lined up along the walls, and there was a chart with a list of diving do's and don'ts. Lucy opened the door and put her head in. "Mateo, is Josey around?"

"No, he's out." He threw her a big grin and went back to writing. Like Josey, he was friendly but taciturn. Lucy shut the door.

Up on the hill a few yards away was another building. It was where Josey lived: a simple two-room cement structure with a thatched roof and a porch that overlooked the ocean. Two wicker chairs and a small table rested like a still-life painting underneath the porch eaves. Lucy and Freddy went over to the house and knocked on the door. No answer. Lucy sighed. "I guess he really isn't here." They began their short walk back to the main thoroughfare of the island by way of the road to the shop. "I never knew this road went to Squash Beach or anywhere besides the dive shop," Lucy said.

"It's because it loops behind Josey's house and disappears," Freddy remarked, adding, "Tomorrow, we should try looking for the lost spring again. I mean, I didn't even really look for it."

"The road makes it quick," Lucy replied, only this time we'll bring more water and food."

"We could use towels too."

"And a machete for breaking open coconuts."

"Good. What fun."

They entered the main road about halfway between the church and the Beach Lodge. When they went by the colorful houses, they spotted Liam in the window of a purple house. The curtain blowing one way then another revealed his face and three other local men sitting at a table. A dominoes game was taking place, and every time one of them slammed a piece down, they shouted something like, "Puppa jeezas!" or "Wah mek!" When Liam yelled, "Muggins!" they heard the tumbling sound of dominoes hitting the floor and then a lot of scuffling. There was a bottle of whiskey on the table and several empty beers.

"I wonder if he ever eats?" Lucy questioned.

"Speaking of food, I'm famished." Freddy was looking at a coconut tree on the side of the road. "I hope it's coconut conch soup to-night. No, I take that back. I'd like a steak."

"I bet it's snapper," Lucy said, prying her eyes away from Liam in the window.

"I'm not betting. But then my luck has changed. I bet grouper."

They shook.

Once at the Beach Lodge, they went their separate ways to clean up for dinner.

Chapter
14

Porch Bar and Grill

By the time Lucy walked onto the restaurant porch of the Porch Bar and Grill, the sun had set. An Irish couple was already seated on the couch talking to a French woman and her poodle. The single twenty-watt bulb caused their coloring to be sepia. Lucy said, "Hello," and went into the restaurant's kitchen.

Aurora was stirring a coconut concoction on the stove. The intense smell galvanized Lucy's hunger, and her mouth immediately salivated. Just as thirsty as she was hungry, she put a couple of lempiras in a rusty can that was labeled *beer money*, opened the refrigerator, and took a cold Salva Vida out. Screwing the top off, she took a gulp, swallowed, and stifled a burp in order to ask, "What's for dinner?"

Aurora turned halfway around, her usually pale skin red from the heat. She had lizard eyes and a hooked, pinched nose. Her mouth was almost always open, revealing a bad front tooth, blackened and outlined with gold. Lucy assumed she was probably in her fifties but then was not sure. She did not know her well. "Coconut fish stew," Aurora replied, her tone crabby. She went back to stirring.

"What kind of fish?"

"Red snapper." Aurora did not bother to turn back around.

"Yum," Lucy mumbled, smiling that she had won the bet with Freddy about dinner. Leaning back against the refrigerator, she took another sip of beer, this time more tempered. Staring at Aurora's thin, sleeveless shirt, she watched her loose underarm skin flap back and forth with each vigorous stir, the bubbling broth the only sound to be heard.

Lucy thought about what she knew of the woman in front of her. She was married to Dan. The couple was from Australia and owned the place. Aurora seemed always to be working; scrubbing, mopping, and cooking, along with weeding the grounds that were nothing but weeds. She even had a helper, a young local girl named Betty who was the granddaughter of Florence, Arnoldo's part-time cook. But it didn't seem to matter that Aurora had help. The work seemed endless. Lucy didn't quite understand the need to scrub so much. But then, Lucy had never even owned a car, let alone a house that seconded as a restaurant. It also occurred to her that she may never want to own anything ever.

The dim lighting in the all-white kitchen was pacifying. It reminded Lucy of being at home and watching her mother cook. It was a comforting feeling, and she had no desire to rush back to the porch.

She began to entertain herself with a compare-and-contrast exercise, something her English professors in college loved to have them do when analyzing two characters in a novel. She decided to compare Lilly, the owner of the No Name restaurant, and Aurora, another restaurateur, and jotted down facts in her mind: two middle-aged women working hard to serve the public, neither one particularly attractive, both overweight, and as far as she could tell, neither one had children—yet one of them was unhappy and dour, and the other vibrant and jubilant. Why? Unable to answer the question, Lucy let her eyes roam around the kitchen and into a little side room. Spotting an archaic-looking transistor radio, she asked, "What do you use the radio for?"

Aurora turned her head slightly, eyeing Lucy from the corner of her left eye. "Still here? Now and then *yah gotta* talk to the outside world." Lucy didn't really hear what Aurora said because the bumblebee clip pulling back Aurora's black and gray hair had caught her attention. She wondered why someone Aurora's age would wear such a clip. Ruminating over Lilly's and Aurora's lives, Lucy couldn't help but wonder if she might resemble one or both when she became elderly, and would she wear a bumblebee clip too? Although it was very hard to fathom being so old.

Hearing voices in the yard, Lucy looked out the window. Dan was in the yard drinking a beer standing next to Mateo. Mateo was pointing a garden shovel at the ground while talking and shaking his head, then he laughed. Dan had a rake in his hand. The front of his shirt was wet and plastered to his belly. He also had soggy, damp armpits. His dark, thinning hair was matted to his head. He was giving Mateo a mean look.

Dan seemed to be working all the time too, Lucy thought. But Mateo also worked a lot. Her mind turned to comparing and contrasting the men. She thought about how Mateo smiled when greeting people. And then there was Dan, who muttered to himself when digging holes and pulling up weeds. Dan also had a hard time saying "hello" to people who greeted him when passing by.

Sighing, Lucy took several sips of her beer and went back to watching Aurora cook. She was now tossing herbs into the mix. She had fat folds on her back that were enhanced by the tight bib ties. Lucy resumed her compare-and-contrast chart about Aurora and Lilly and added Dan to Aurora's side and Mateo to Lilly's. Under *compare*, she put *they all are trying to make money*. Under *contrast*, she put *Aurora and Dan lack joy while Lilly and Mateo have joy* and left her thoughts of them at that. Chuckling, she shook her head, thinking about her mediocre grades in school.

When Aurora turned around again and looked at Lucy, she felt a little foolish that she was still standing there. Thinking she should say something, she asked, "Where's Betty?"

"Diarrhea." Aurora went back to stirring.

Lucy mulled over the mixed fragrance of spices and fish and wondered if there was something in the food that caused Betty's illness. Aurora, as though reading her mind, said, "She ate a bad clam from her yard." Betty lived in one of the colorful row houses.

Putting her empty beer into a rack to be recycled, Lucy threw more money into the can, grabbed another beer, and left. Walking onto the porch, she looked for the Italians. She wanted to practice their accent. Freddy had arrived and was over in a corner sitting with the Irish couple. They seemed to be having an intense conversation. His beer was almost gone. She wondered where he had gotten it and assumed from Ernesto. Freddy had a button-down shirt with palm trees on it, his hair was brushed back, and he looked clean and tidy. A completely different person, Lucy thought.

Not seeing the Italians, she let her eyes roam throughout the room wondering where she wanted to sit. Listening, Lucy heard the French woman, who was next to the Irish and Freddy, tell a scuba diving tale. It was fun to hear the diver's stories about near misses with sharks; the crazy barracuda-staring contests; the multitudes of parrot, clown, and angel fish; and the occasional panic attack. Near death by drowning, the possibility of the bends, and the lack of air mayhem were also often spoken about and intriguing. Lucy sat down next to the French woman on a weathered couch draped in a sheet that needed to be washed.

The French woman's black toy poodle was on her lap. The woman was telling a story about a tiger shark and a sunken sailboat with a safe inside that was thought to have money. The Irish couple and Freddy were quasi-listening. The Irish couple said they had seen the same shark and the boat and looked bored. Freddy, who had picked the label off his beer, got up and went into the kitchen even though the French woman was not finished. Anyone who had been on the island for more than a week knew the safe and the money was made up to provide intrigue to the island and hence, one of the lures of taking diving classes, along with the famous coral reef. Lucy sighed, thinking the lost spring was most likely another fictitious tale, but she liked the idea of it so didn't care.

The Irish woman watched Freddy walk away and shifted in her seat. Interrupting the French woman, she said, "Sharks remind me of children, which is why I don't want them." She had kinky, brassy hair and an alabaster complexion splattered with rusty freckles. Although she was in her mid-thirties, her lips and cheeks were already sinking into her mouth. Lucy wondered if in ten years or so her cheeks would be eating her mouth too.

"I don't see how sharks make you think of kids," the Irish man said, picking his nose and flicking it onto the weed lawn.

The French woman laughed. "But they are. I have two. When they want money, they circle me into a little hole until they get a chunk."

Lucy thought about her parents and if they would have the same sentiments as the Irish and French women if she called home and

125

asked for money. Possibly? She dismissed the notion. She then thought to tell the group about looking for a lost spring on the other side of the island but stopped short of the first word out. Something about it seemed like it should be just Freddy and her story for the time being. Besides, what if one of them wanted to go there and look with them? They might go swimming in the pool. Still disturbed about the road, the less newcomers knew about Squash Beach, the better.

When the Italians arrived, Lucy smiled and said, "*Buono sera.*" They smiled back. One of the boys threw her a kiss. They seemed already drunk. They had two bottles of tequila, both half-full. Since the Aussies only sold beer, water, and Coca-Cola, it was fine to bring wine or hard liquor (however, no one on the island sold wine).

The Italians talked loudly, their hand gestures causing them to spill the liquor that was in their Dixie cups. Sitting on stools by a Mayan statue with a large penis, they began pointing and laughing at it. They took the baby conch shells that were on a nearby shelf and lined them along the penis. Taking turns, they tried to blow them off and made a lot of huffing and puffing noises mixed with spit in doing so. Lucy had wanted to talk to them tonight, but they seemed too preoccupied. When Freddy sat down next to them to take a turn at the game, Lucy laughed. It was all so silly.

The sound of a bottle tipping onto the floor caught Lucy's attention. Over by the far rail, someone was asleep on the only lounge chair on the porch. Whoever it was had pulled a towel, splattered with pink flamingos, over their head. The rest of the person's body exposed, displayed colorful Jams and an opened okra button-down shirt; the man had a white chest with fuzzy blond-red hair around his nipples. An arm tangled by several empty beer bottles on the floor. One had tipped over, creating a foamy puddle. "Liam," Lucy mumbled. She wondered if he was ever sober.

As though he felt her eyes on him, he reached up and pulled a corner of the towel off his face, revealing an eye. It peered at her like a dead fish. Lucy quickly looked away. Refocusing her attention on the Irish woman; she listened to her tell a story about a wayward brother back home and his obsession with old ladies and their money. "I have ten sisters and one brother. My mother's womb is like a deflated bean-bag chair." Lucy made a face. Glancing back over at Liam, she saw he had taken the towel completely off his head. He was gazing at the shabby backyard.

Lucy looked too but more at the jungle. Beyond the realm of the porch, the tree line was distant and dark, and there were bats sweeping through the twilight. Butterflies, white, blue, and pink, fluttered and weaved around mealy bushes. Planting her eyes on Liam, she watched him shift, then pull the flamingo towel up to his chin. Then he turned back around and latched his eyes onto hers. "Wood nymphs dancing," Liam sighed. His accent was lyrical and at the same time stunted, each word like a chopping block. The Irish couple and the French woman quieted themselves and looked over at Liam, too.

"One of my fucked-up brothers writes poetry in jail," the Irish woman said to him.

"I would have liked to have been a poet. However, my parents think being an artist is just another excuse for doing nothing." His words were heavy, he then sighed and said with mirth, "I think without art, we are doing nothing but dry humping each other."

The group laughed except for the Italians. They were too preoccupied with lining up the conch shells again to blow off.

"My Fifi," the French woman said, stroking the dog. "She likes to hump cushions and table legs. I should teach her to paint. You know, paw-paint. She might stop such unattractive behaviors."

Again, the group laughed.

"Tomorrow. Tomorrow I will become a better man," Liam said, grasping the towel and throwing it over his face. Lucy felt an uneasiness grip the air. It seemed no one knew what to make of his statement. Even the Italians had stopped blowing on the conch shells, Liam's drama a different source of amusement. But as nothing else was said, the group went back to chatting and playing.

Freddy sat down next to Lucy on the couch; his weight caused her to bump into the air. "I got all the conchs off the penis with only three blows," Freddy said.

Lucy tapped his beer with hers. "Cheers."

"We won't get married." The Irish man's voice resonated in the air. He seemed to be talking louder than usual.

"You see, in Ireland, they don't allow divorce," the Irish woman added.

"I guess if you do marry, 'till death do us part' may take on a whole new meaning," Freddy said. He gave a chuckle, and so did the French woman; her poodle made an odd gurgle, but both Irish remained solemn.

Lucy refocused on Liam. He was like a scab or a pussy pimple that compels one to pick at it. Once again, he had one eye peeking out from his towel. "Creepy," she mumbled, glancing down at the floor.

"My dear child, be a love and get a thirsty fellow a beer," Liam's soft voice spoke to her.

But Lucy pretended not to hear him. He grunted and got up. Straightening his clothes with fingers spread, he swayed, then gained a sense of balance by grabbing the porch railing. He stood for a moment staring at the entrance to the kitchen as though to reach it would be like running a marathon. Then he pointed at it with an *I got this* expression and walked with unsteady legs to the doorway and disappeared.

Freddy, who was still sitting next to Lucy, glanced toward the stairs. Lucy looked too. It was the woman from the mail boat. She was standing at the top. Her presence demanded attention, Lucy thought, but then any new nuance entering the room always did. It was as though they were always looking for a new diversion.

Lucy squinted, trying to see her better in the dull lighting. The mailwoman was younger and prettier than she had remembered. She guessed her age to be late twenties or early thirties. Standing upright, her body lean and solid, she had on beige cargo shorts that fell to her knees. Her shirt was a man's white T-shirt, the loose collar around the neck exposing well-formed cleavage. Her shoulder-length dark hair was messily clipped back from her face. An oval face with light eyes. Lucy noted that she had a mysterious dark aura that surrounded her as though she were haunted by something. *Maybe she is French*, Lucy thought, *or Italian*. But then she looked over at the Italians; they seemed gauche and plain compared to her. Lucy watched the woman walk toward the kitchen as though she knew the routine. *But then, of course, she would*, Lucy thought, wondering how long she'd been a mailwoman in the area.

Liam was on his way out of the kitchen with a beer in his hand and bumped into her.

"Pardon me," he said, then paused as though not sorry at all and took hold of her arm. "You! I think you have something of mine."

Her face appeared shocked at first, eyes widening, then nearly shutting with annoyance. She pulled her arm away from his.

Blocking her way with his arms across the entrance, he growled, "I was trying to do some reading in that insufferable beach room. Key gone. You wouldn't know anything about that now?"

"No, I don't," she answered, trying to get by him. He grabbed her arm again. "Fuck! I had to bash open my valise. And, well...my folder is missing. Give it back!" His lips were pursed with white lines, while every muscle on his face bulged with anger. Eleanor glared at him and took a step away, then once again yanked her arm out of his grip. She looked like she might run. Liam lunged at her with his hands out front and arms wide. He miscalculated where she was, missed, lost his balance, and fell onto his knees. His beer jarred out of his grip and skittled along the floor.

When he tried to scramble back up with his hands flung out to get hold of her, he misjudged where the doorframe was located and slammed his hands against it, then his head. He crumpled to the floor and lay dazed on his back looking up at the ceiling. "I think I may have dislodged an intervertebral disc," he said in a calm voice, then reached out at Eleanor's ankles. Although his strike was quick, he missed and hit his hand on the doorframe again. Eleanor backed herself over to the steps and stopped. She looked at Liam on the floor. Lucy saw an upturn at the corner of her mouth. She was smiling, Lucy thought, and wondered why she even stayed. Why didn't she run? When a moody scowl encompassed her face, Lucy saw her breathe deeply and become calm. *I bet she dives; stop, breath, and think*, Lucy thought, and turned to see where Freddy was to make a bet. He was a yard away, intensely watching the scene.

Then Aurora walked out of the kitchen doorway and onto the porch. She appeared unaware of the small tempest that had just taken place. Her work face on and focused on a covered tin container in her hands, as though trying not to spill, she mindlessly stepped over Liam and went over to the mailwoman. "Here you go, Eleanor. Lots of tasty stuff in this soup. Now, if Juan wants bread, stop off at the No Name.

It's not open. But you know what to do; just knock. They have loaves of coco de pan." She then spotted Liam on the floor. "What are you doing down there?"

"Resting," he said.

"Well, don't look up my shift." Aurora stepped back over him and returned to the kitchen.

Several people on the porch chuckled, including Lucy and Freddy.

Eleanor, with her pot of food, began to walk down the steps. Lucy wanted to know her nationality and rushed over. In Spanish, using what she perceived to be an authentic Italian accent, she said, "*Buenas noches. Soy Lucy. Estoy de Italia.*" To make the whole accent more complete, she threw her hands in the air. This made the Italians snicker, but they said nothing to refute her claim on their nationality.

"Eleanor," she said, then leaned in toward Lucy and smiled. "I'm an American."

One of the Italian boys exploded with laughter; in English, he remarked, "My name is Waldo. I am a mermaid and live in the ocean." Lucy threw him a dirty look as if to say, *Shut up.*

Eleanor smiled and once again turned to leave.

"So, you're not Greek or French?" Lucy asked, speaking English because she forgot to speak Spanish.

"No," Eleanor said with her back to Lucy.

Lucy sighed with disappointment. "We thought you might be Greek."

Eleanor ignored her comment and kept going. She disappeared into the night.

Freddy, who had crept over to the steps, stood by Lucy and mumbled, "I think she's lying. Did you see how she pushed Liam to the ground? I'm positive she's Greek."

Lucy chuckled. "Eleanor didn't push him; Liam fell." Then, amused, she added, "I'm not giving you a pilito unless she admits to being Greek. Oh, and it's snapper tonight. You owe me a pilito."

Just as Freddy handed Lucy her winnings, Liam jumped up and scattered his half-empty beer bottle across the floor. He charged off the porch by leaping over the steps. He made a wobbly landing on the grass. He straightened himself up and ran into the darkness.

"I wonder what this is all about?" Freddy said.

"I bet she has his folder?" Lucy said and held out her hand.

"Why would she do that? I bet she doesn't. I bet he lost it due to being such an enormous drunk," Freddy remarked.

They shook hands.

Chapter
15

Josey Wales

Josey Wales kicked his legs over the side of the bed and sat. He had slept well, a pleasurable reprieve from his restless sleep the night before. Hunched over, he rubbed his brow, eyes, and down to his mouth; yawned; then lifted himself off the sunken mattress. Naked, he walked over to the only other piece of furniture in the small all-white room, a spindly, wooden chair that held neatly folded pants, a shirt, underwear, and socks. Leaning against the chair was a beige rucksack, his toilet kit on top of it. His leather loafers were by the front door. When he came into the house last night, he replaced them with indoor shoes, cushy slippers.

Josey picked up his toilet kit, but when a dove perched on the windowsill peeked in and cooed, it caught his attention. He met its tiny round black eyes with his. They stayed mindful of each other as seconds passed, and the bird flew away. Leaning his head out the window, he followed the dove's swirls up the courtyard walls. It finally settled along the roofline with others of its kind. *Peaceful and beautiful,* he thought, then put his slippers on and gathered his clothes and toilet kit to bring into the bathroom.

The bathroom was small and beige, and the shower lacked a curtain along with a showerhead. The water flowed out like a garden hose, and when it hit his back, it splattered everywhere. He got out and tossed his clothes into the hall to keep them dry. When he got back into the shower, the water had become cold, so he fiddled with the electric heater attached to the spout. It electrocuted him with tiny stings. He stepped back against the wall and shrugged. His aunt had oodles of money but did not want to advertise it so never repaired a thing. When the warm water began to flow, he soaped up and stood under the cascading heat with his hands on the tiled wall, head down, and eyes closed. He let the water beat on his shoulders and back. His thoughts were momentarily empty, as he was enjoying his respite from the world and its worries, until his aunt banged on the door to scold him about his excessive water usage. He turned it off. A rough air-dried towel hung on the back of the door. He wiped the water from his body and cleaned the fog off the mirror to stare at himself. He noticed his dark roots had started to give him a two-toned appearance. When he had first dyed his hair, he didn't like the look. Although he had blue eyes that went well with yellow, aesthetically, his olive skin clashed. Taking a Q-tip and a bottle of bleach from his toilet kit, he dabbed his dark roots. His aunt and Oggi didn't like the blond job either, but purple or blue hair would bring too much attention to him. And seeing how he needed something to alter his appearance, and plastic surgery was out of the question, going blond was the way to go.

He took his time shaving, using light strokes along his firm jawline. When he finished, he rubbed his neck and twisted his chin right to left to make sure he had been thorough. Except for the blond hair, he liked how he looked, classically handsome with strong, interesting features: angled nose, a sensual mouth, steady discerning eyes that easily smiled and showed interest with ease. His six-foot stature often drew stares from men and women. But since he wasn't trying to look his best, he had taken on a slouch when he walked about in public. When in the city, he usually wore baggy T-shirts and jeans bought in the cheap clothing markets. But not today. He was on a mission. He needed to have his picture taken and for a certain man to do him a favor. Josey straightened himself up and said, "Much better," then spoke soothing words: "You'll be okay. This too shall pass." He then tapped right below his neck. For years he had worn a solid gold locket that held pictures of his parents. From all the upsets and moving from one country to another, they had become the only photos he had of them. The locket was lost at some point at the orphanage and his parents' images had begun to fade; it deeply saddened him.

He shrugged and applied a good layer of Old Spice under his arms and a touch of aftershave on his face. The streets of Tegucigalpa would become hot and suffocating once the asphalt heated up and the smog grew thick. Just the idea of fumes, dust, noise, and sweltering humidity made him want to return as quickly as possible to the island. Josey dressed in a crisp cream-colored button-down shirt and dark gray slacks, then went into the kitchen.

His aunt had left the house, and there was a note tucked beneath his plate of beans and eggs. Folded into the note was a large jagged, key that could not be duplicated. He placed it in his pocket and poured himself coffee from the metal pot on the table, then topped it off with hot milk from a small pitcher. He sat, took a sip, and one bite of the meal. He wasn't hungry. As he read the note, he saw that the aunt's instructions were very precise. He got up and went down a flight of steps to a dank, musty basement. When he pulled the chain on the overhead light bulb, small black vermin ran beneath boxes and into holes. The walls were white plaster and had started to crumble onto the cement floor; a dribble of water flowed in from a corner. He let his eyes roam over a broken chair and several boxes and shelves. Then he spotted what he was looking for: several colorful woolen blankets. According to his aunt's directions, what he wanted was hidden underneath them.

He tossed the blankets aside and stepped back. The safe was a be-hemoth thick-metal box, black with gold inlay. Josey wondered where she had gotten such a grand piece. Chuckling, he smiled; his aunt was one of the most resourceful people he knew. Leaning in, he inserted the key and turned it. The bolts clicked and the safe door opened. He looked over the interior contents: to the back were gold bars piled in rows and stacked to the top. In a corner, gold and silver coins. Bundles of twenties, fifties, and hundred-dollar American bills were banded and stacked, taking up a third of the interior. In a plastic Ziplock bag in front of it all were passports and a gold watch.

He took the Ziplock bag out and opened it. He spent a moment fondling the watch. It was his father's. The king of Spain had given it to him, although the Ramoses now claimed it as theirs. He dropped it back into the bag and took out a burgundy booklet with the coat of arms of a crown held by two griffins. It was his Dutch passport. Thumbing through the pages, he saw the stamps of Italy, Spain, Germany, Kenya, Morocco, Holland, and Chile. Places he had visited, whereas Chile was where he was born and lived off and on with his parents. He then turned to his picture. His youthful self: the hair dark, the eyes curious, the face plumper. The name Heraldo Pinola Alvares Vander Gar de Unias in bold lettering had been his birth name, a name he could never use again. It made him sad. His mother's side of the family, Vander Gar, allowed him to be a Dutch citizen. One of the few passports he had that rang true. Now, he needed to have it doctored: the picture changed and the dates. He placed the expired passport into his back pocket.

He also took a bundle of dollars from the stash—hundred-dollar bills that added up to thousands—then relocked the safe, covered it up with the blankets, and went back up to the kitchen. As instructed, he put the key in a box under the sink that was full of sand and said 'rat poison,' then sat back down to finish his breakfast. But all he could do was push the food around. He glanced at the clock on the wall; it was still early, seven o'clock in the morning. The man he needed to see wasn't up yet. He was also mad at himself for the new name he had chosen. Josey Wales was hardly a Dutch name. He had picked it after watching *The Outlaw Josey Wales* on a black-and-white TV in a hotel room a year ago. Hiding from his pursuers, the gritty Josey Wales character had fascinated him. He could relate to the loss of family and being called an outlaw. Although the idea of revenge crossed his mind from time to time, overall, he found the emotion a waste of time— better to move on with one's life than to ruin it by chasing assholes. Yet, he did enjoy watching Josey shoot and kill his enemies. For a whole year, he had been going by the name Josey Wales. People knew him on the island by that name. It would have to do.

He placed the money and passport inside a small satchel and walked out of the house onto a busy street. Cars and buses had started their commute. The bluster of honks, shouts, and engine exhaust had him pick up his pace. He briskly walked toward the Plaza Morazán because it was near his appointment. He wanted to sit under the trees and read a book. He had brought with him *Los Detectives Salvajes*, by Roberto Bolaño. The book was about a gang of poets who referred to themselves as *Visceral Realists*. It was a piece of fiction highly relatable to his life or one that he perceived himself to live. The bohemian lifestyle was appealing; the idea of tasting and breathing poetry, a magnificent way to live. He sat under a jacaranda tree with beautiful orange and yellow flowers. As he read, he could smell the tree's floral essence, and his present worries disappeared. Having written poems all his life, he thought perhaps he would start up again. The island was the perfect place for him with its languid days and peaceful nights. He read a few more pages, and his mood gained levity. *The world is my oyster*, he said to himself, shutting the book. And the future? He thrummed his thumbs on the ground. *One day at a time, one day at a time.*

At 9:45, he left for his appointment. He walked a block and turned left down a narrow street to a mustard-colored stucco building. Josey went in the front door and up three flights of stairs to a dingy office filled with papers and the smell of ink. A woman sitting at a wooden desk was painting her nails; she looked up and greeted him: "Señor Guiza is waiting for you." She nodded toward a shut door. Josey opened the door and walked in. A man with a large forehead and small hands sat behind a disheveled gray metal desk. He motioned for Josey to sit, which he did, in the only other chair in the room, a disintegrating faux-leather armchair, but not before handing Señor Guiza the expired Dutch passport. "I need it to be up to date, a new photo, and change the name to Josey Wales."

The man laughed. "How about Vander Wales? Or Van Wales? Much more believable."

Josey didn't find him funny. Nothing was funny to him when it came to the details of getting caught or escaping. He knew the passport that gave him British citizenship would have been better for his new Wild West name, but it was gone. The police had confiscated it when he fled Guatemala with his aunt and nephew. But the man had a point. To put a Dutch prefix in front of Wales would make the name much more believable.

The forger and Josey stared at each other, as though contemplating a bank robbery. "Okay," Josey finally said. "Van Wales."

"We need to take a photo. Are you going to remain a blond?"

"Yes."

"You could shave it."

Josey shrugged.

Smiling, he asked, "Same birth date?"

"Yes."

Josey and the man spent another ten minutes bargaining over the price. A deposit of $500 was put on the table. He would pay another $1,500 when he came to pick it up. The quickest he could have the passport completed, a week.

"How much to have it completed by noon, today?" Josey had a diving business to run, along with the possibility of having to leave the country before the week's end.

"Five hundred dollars more." The man's upper lip curled when he spoke.

"Done." Josey left the office. Slightly jumpy from his dealings with such a dubious character, he had no desire to return to his aunt's house just yet. He went to his favorite café that was located on a quiet side street of the city. The cubist mural on the wall and spider plants were fun along with tranquil. He sat down at a table by an open French window and ordered a café con leche and pan dulce. Opening his book, he sipped coffee, munched on the sweet pastry, and read. With the light morning breeze caressing his face, Josey lost himself in the world of *Visceral Reality* poetics, once again.

A few hours later, he picked the passport up. It was good. The man had been worth the money. Horns honking, dust, and exhaust spewed in his face; by the time he reached the house, his mind was already on the fresh air and cleansing seas of the island.

"*Hijo,*" Yena said as he walked into the house. "The passport?"

"All set."

Yena's round face beamed with delight. Her padded eyelids, thick salt-and-pepper hair, and diminutive stature spoke of her Chilean mountain origins. She wore a house dress and flat leather sandals. Her native thick woolen skirt, cotton top, and colorful vest she never wore anymore. It was better to fit in.

Josey held her in his arms and gave her a long hug. "My last name is Van Wales, now," he said, smiling. This made her laugh.

"Such a silly name you chose this time around." She lit the stove to reheat the coffee and milk. She took a newspaper out of her satchel and tossed it on the table. "The cousin who was with Liam died in Copan a few weeks ago. They had been drinking with some foreign girls, and he was bitten by a snake."

Josey picked the paper up. The article about the cousin's death mentioned a man named Liam Titlemen. He smiled and looked at his aunt. "He's using his grandmother's name instead of his mother's, Ramos." The article revealed that both the cousin and Titlemen were on a mission to find fugitives who had absconded with a Chilean family's fortune. However, the fugitives' names were not mentioned, nor were their photos in the paper. "Interesting, they didn't mention us in the paper, this time."

"If you read more, it seems Liam didn't want to scare the criminals away," the aunt said.

"To think we had Sunday meals with that family." Josey leaned back in his chair and looked over at his aunt. "If he sees me, he'll know who I am. Blond or not." As he bit his lower lip, his body grew heavy. "Do you know where Liam is? Did you hear any scuttle from your busybody contacts?"

"He's on the island." Her tone was almost a whisper. "We could pull everything together and leave tonight."

Silence.

"Is it just him there?"

"I think so."

Josey placed his hands on top of his head to think. "Maybe he *won't* recognize me. If he doesn't, good. Life will continue as usual. If he does, I've got the boat. I'll take off and head over to La Ceiba. You can meet me there with Oggie, and.... Where do we want to go?"

She smiled. "Australia. Remember? We decided it would be our next place if...well..." Her voice trailed off. She walked over and hugged him from behind.

"We can go up to Belize. Fly out of there. Hell, I don't know. Australia's awfully far away."

He felt like crawling back into bed, but then anger took over, and his energy returned. He took a deep breath and welcomed his aunt's kiss on his cheek and returned her gesture by giving her hands a light squeeze. She rested her hand on his shoulder. "The more I think about it...Liam's a drunk. And drunks make lots of mistakes." Then she laughed. "God is a big game changer. Call me tomorrow with an update. He may have fallen into the ocean and sunk to his death." She nodded to the boat radio that was on the counter. The coffee and milk bubbling on the stove, she walked over to it and poured each of them a cup. "He'll botch this up," she continued, adding, "Papa Ramos will be disgusted with his son. The search will end for a while. Let's just hope the old man dies. His wife is already an invalid from drink."

"I doubt their children will let it go."

"The letters I get from home tell me that the eldest wants nothing to do with it. Liam has been dragged in because he relies on their money. The cousin also thought he was entitled to what's ours, along with a consulate fellow in Mexico City who claims to be a relative of theirs."

"What about Dori?"

"He's the one who sold us out in El Puente. When you were at the orphanage. He was living on his sailboat at the club. Did you know that? Did you see him?"

"No, but then, he's younger and I wasn't around much. Hell, they sent him off to school at an early age, too. They must have given him a picture of me. Did the letters from home tell you this?"

"It's in the paper."

"Really." Josey read the rest of the article. "It says he saw us, and he informed the police."

"He's a playboy like Liam. No doubt sailing around and stumbled across us. According to relatives back home, he's missing now."

"What?"

"Dori went off with a woman and is missing. Maybe drowned. Let's hope so."

Josey tapped his finger on the table and rose. "He just doesn't want to be found. When he gets bored, he'll come out of hiding." His mood was pensive and techy. "I need to go."

They hugged. Yena crossed herself as she watched him walk out the door.

Chapter
16

The Storm

The late-night storm had kept Lucy and Freddy up into the wee hours of the morning. It didn't bother either one that they didn't get much sleep. The dazzling flashes of light and clatter of the sky drew them in, mesmerized by the wild ride. The tide had come up over the rocks during the night and in through the back door of the No Name. The cigar-rolling business toward the left, sheltered by lumpy boulders, was perfectly dry. The restaurant's interior was drenched with seaweed and puddles. Freddy swished his mouth around in a circle and said, "Another good scrubbing."

Lilly greeted them with wet, spongy pink slippers on that squished when she walked. The mole on her chin seemed larger. She appeared unfazed by the storm, wiped a table off, tossed a few bits of seaweed aside, and served them coffee, eggs, and beans. Lucy also bought a baggie of three cigars. She imagined herself smoking one of the thick nibs while drinking a beer after dowsing at Squash Beach.

She tossed a stogie at Freddy.

He smelled it and frowned. "Fishy." They both had a good laugh imagining cigars packaged as "Tangy, fish-tasting smokes" or "Aromatic clam-flavored" or "Low-tide delight."

Chuckling, they split the bill and headed off toward town for supplies. They were feeling fun, and life was airy and full of extraordinary promises. As they headed back down the beach, it was with forceful, vibrant strides, something very unusual. Lucy laughed; gazed at the bright, cloudless day; and said, "It's a cutesy-poo sky, not blue." Freddy found the word *cutesy-poo* to be too stupid and renamed the sky *lollygag*. Lucy liked the word *lollygag* and agreed.

"If we are going to play with words, I think we should stick to calling what we do either *codswallop,* which seems to be what it really is, or just plain *dowsing*. Much more professional," he stated, adding, "It's already hideously hot."

Lucy looked at him puzzled, opened her umbrella and broke a leaf off a tree to fan herself. For the time being, she let the whole word choice for their work sit idle. Sighing, she said, "They're monks that can imagine themselves hot when it's cold. Maybe we can imagine ourselves cold when it's hot?"

"I don't think I have the discipline," Freddy replied. His feet were already dragging, and Lucy noticed a bend in his back like he was slumping. She wanted to tell him to stand up straight, but then he might not look like Freddy.

"I can't focus long enough. Cold to hot, hot to cold wouldn't work for me either," she said, still fanning herself.

When they came upon the row of two-room houses, they paused to comment. It appeared everyone was asleep. The windows still had their curtains drawn. They also saw how the tide had washed over the road in places, creating ruts and squiggles. Broken beer bottles and multicolored wrappers were now part of the landscape, which made the place look dirty and unkempt. It bothered them, and they both wondered if there was a cleanup crew for the streets like there was for the beach. "Probably not," Freddy said, and they both began picking up wrappers, pieces of boat rope, and bottle tops until their hands couldn't hold anymore. Not wanting to carry the garbage, they put it neatly by a rock.

"If we remember, we should pick it up later and throw it away," Lucy remarked.

They had only passed a few houses when Lucy realized her sneakers were untied. She stopped and sat on a half-rotted stump to re-tie them. Beetles and tiny white bugs were pilfering the dead wood. Lucy watched them carrying away pieces as she haphazardly laced her sneakers. When Freddy belched, she looked up. With his lips tight against his teeth and his eyes slits that were darting around the periphery with swift, panicked glances, he mumbled something about breakfast giving his stomach a pinch. Spotting the communal outhouse on the dock, he walked briskly toward it, then ran. He whipped the door open, entering; it slapped shut behind him. Lucy frowned when she saw the silhouettes of Freddy's turds fall into the ocean. It occurred to her that swimming anywhere on this island could be unsanitary.

"Don't worry," Freddy said as he walked back toward her, buttoning his shorts. "Squash Beach is on the other side of the island. The fish will have eaten it all by then."

They continued down the road with short steps and sweat beading on their foreheads. Lucy's armpits felt slimy, and she wiped them with the dry part of her shirt. The sun, a hot ball of fire in the sky, had awoken the whine of insects. The sound seemed louder and tighter, and both Lucy and Freddy found themselves talking louder too. Stopping by a chartreuse house, Lucy said, "I wonder if they use fans. I mean with the curtains drawn."

"The air must be watery and stinky," Freddy said.

Treading her eyes up and down the sides of the houses, Lucy wondered if the roofs on the houses were solid and if the rain had gotten in last night. She also noticed lots of white clams entangled in seaweed in the rocks below. Several were opened, piled high by the wooden posts. "I bet big water rats live under those houses."

They began to walk again and passed a purple house. A man with eyes that looked like fried eggs and hands that seemed too large for him was standing on the house porch sipping a beer. He stared at them as though suspicious of their intentions. Freddy and Lucy smiled and waved. He nodded back, flat and disinterested.

Moving along, Freddy puckered his lips and twisted his curly hair into a bun on top of his head. Lucy thought he looked like a carnival lady but kept her thoughts for later. Lucy then randomly brought up the notion of work because it seemed not many people were up yet.

"Fishermen," Freddy stated. "They got up early and left already."

"Not everyone can be fishing. I wonder if Josey still is?"

"I don't know why he would be; he already has a job." Sniffing the air, he continued, "Now, people eat the fish. And drink and make babies. There is a lot going on here that we don't see," Freddy said, then went on to say, "Looking from the outside in again, I don't know if we will ever really know what most of these islanders are up to."

"I prefer it that way," Lucy remarked. "I don't want to be looking from the inside out. Something about it seems unsettling, like a trap." She paused here to look at the store in the near distance. "Do you think Fabio minds living in a cage?"

"Would you want to live in a cage?"

"No." Lucy sighed and stopped. Looking off at the bay, her eyes caught sight of the mail boat still docked. "I guess the storm kept them from leaving last night."

"Possibly they were never planning to leave."

As they both looked closer, they saw Eleanor walk out into the cockpit. She had a mug in her hand and was talking to someone in the pilothouse. When she threw her head back, they could hear exuberant laughter bellowing from the boat. She stopped to say something again, then went over to the gunwale and leaned against it to look out toward land. She stared right at them.

"Do you think she sees us?" Freddy mumbled, waving. Eleanor waved back at them.

"I guess so."

"How can we find out if she took the folder or not?" Lucy asked, still looking at Eleanor, who was still staring at them.

"Not sure. Possibly a touchy subject."

Freddy and Lucy, only feet from the store, walked over to Fabio. Lucy cooed, "Good morning sweet bird." There was half of a papaya beneath him, and he was busy snagging pieces of the fruity meat with his beak and making smacking noises. "No greetings back? Are you mad because you're in a cage? Should I set you free?"

"Fuck off," Fabio barked, using a squeaky, static parrot voice.

"What does that mean?" Lucy said.

"He likes his cage," Freddy remarked.

"Doubt it. Bitter."

"Well, don't take him out. He'll probably attack us."

Fabio's flat eyes had black dots circled with white, like a bull's-eye. They looked at Lucy after swallowing, then twitched away. "He seems distant today, possibly due to the storm last night," she said. Taking out a sugar banana from her fanny pack, she peeled it and tapped the bars of the cage again. Fabio twisted his head toward the banana.

"He has a juicy papaya. Why would he want a tiny little banana?" Freddy said.

Lucy ignored Freddy. She then pulled the small fruit away from the bars and hid it in her hand and said to Fabio, "Damn hot."

Fabio cocked his head and peered at her. Lucy repeated "damn hot" several times. On the sixth round, she opened her hand and placed the banana near the bars of the cage, Fabio said, "Damn hot," and squawked. As she shoved the sugar banana through the bars, Fabio thrust his beak forward and nabbed the fruit before it fell to the cage floor.

Freddy laughed. "Gosh, you're good at that."

"He likes mangosteens, best taste for him," a youthful, Carib accent said from the doorway. It was Juanita. She was standing with Bob by her side. Juanita had a plate of rice and beans in one hand and lackadaisically shoved half-filled spoons of the food into her mouth with the other. She wore a plain cotton dress that resembled a school uniform. Her forehead knotted and her eyes bunched together, she appeared perturbed and stated, "Bob wants to come to school with me, but Arnoldo won't let him."

"Now, that's silly. I hated school, and I can't imagine Bob would like it," Freddy said, his tone serious.

Juanita sat down on the stool by the door. Bob moved closer to her, and she fed him some rice.

"Mangosteens?" Lucy inquired. "What are they?"

"They're purple. Small and clumped together. Arnoldo gets them from a beach called Squash." She began to feed Bob more of her food. Using his thick tongue, he licked up the rice and beans from the plate. A fishing rod leaned against the store wall. Juanita put her plate down and grabbed the rod. "Bob and I are going fishing. Would you like to join us?"

Lucy looked over at the church. "It looks like school has started."

They all four peered over at the schoolhouse/church, Fabio too busy eating his papaya to bother. There were around fifteen children milling near the entrance, then one little kid started to run, and they all began to run, around and around the church. At the gin joint, Milly was behind her bar, and two thin men sat at the counter with beers in their hands. They were watching too.

"I'll go later," Juanita said. Bob pulled at her dress to move. They both walked down the path, Juanita with the fishing rod and the donkey with a corner of her dress in his mouth. He was small and his back was even with her waist. Lucy and Freddy watched them walk onto the dock. They also saw that Eleanor had gotten out of the boat. She stood at the end of the dock and was taking off her clothes. Once stripped down to her skivvies, she dove into the water.

"Underwear or a bathing suit?" Freddy said.

"Tough one. Could be a modest Greek. Bathing suit," Lucy said.

They shook and walked into the store.

Chapter
17

Driftwood

Arnoldo was behind the counter, a pipe in his mouth. Swirls of smoke coiled around his head. The whole place smelled of marijuana. With his red-rimmed sunglasses down his nose, he pushed them back up to look at Lucy and Freddy as they entered the shop. "Did my daughter take that donkey to school?"

"No," Lucy said, waving her hand in front of her at the smoke, then sneezed.

"Lucy, you remind me of my dead wife's sister—pretty and prudish." He picked up a letter off the counter, held it to his nose, and gave it a long luxurious whiff. "Freddy, you got mail. Smells female."

Freddy walked over, excited, and took the letter out of Arnoldo's hand. "Gosh, it's from Lyla." His whole appearance seemed to bubble. He sat on the stool by the counter, tore the letter open, and began to read. "She wrote it at the airport in Tegucigalpa while waiting for her flight. Awe, she misses me."

Lucy and Arnoldo briefly stared at Freddy, lost interest, and went about their business, Arnoldo sucking on his pipe while Lucy stood in front of him with a knitted brow. "Do you ride your bike to Squash Beach?" Her tone was rough.

Arnoldo blew out a stream of smoke toward her; she backed away. "This is my island, Lucy. What do you think?"

She bit her lip and looked away, then back at him again, and leaned toward him. "Do you go swimming in a little pool out there with crabs that bite?"

"Lucy, what is this about?"

"Nothing but don't swim in that pool. I'm claiming it."

"Lucy...you can't claim something you don't own."

Freddy looked up from his letter. "We're looking for the lost spring at Squash Beach. It's been fun. I think Lyla will think so too. Yes, I will write her and tell her that I am a dowser now."

Lucy ignored Freddy. It occurred to her that she was happy that Lyla wasn't with them. She felt Lyla might try to change what they were up to, like go on a hike just for a hike, or worse, but not that much worse, hog all of Freddy's attention. She began to gather bags of chips and oranges. The chocolate bars looked good too, and a carton of cookies. She chuckled when she placed Cheese Puffs on the counter with the rest of the goods. For some reason their vibrant orange color seemed silly. She then unwrapped a candy bar and ate it all. For some reason this made her laugh, too. She laughed so hard that she doubled over and dropped the bananas she had in her hands onto the floor. It then occurred to her, she might be high from the pot and stepped farther from Arnoldo into the spice area. By stepping back, she knocked over a stack of limes. Feeling foolish, she began picking them up while laughing uncontrollably.

"What's so funny?" Freddy asked.

Arnoldo, who was watching Lucy with a tiny grin, replied. "So, beefy boy? Eh...you look for the lost spring." Arnoldo took another hit and offered some to Freddy.

He shook his head no. Lucy stopped laughing to respond, "The lost spring." Then burst, "with beefy boy." Her laughter had a high-pitch note to it that made Arnoldo and Freddy chuckle and cringe at the same time.

Then Freddy made a *humph* noise, folded the letter, and put it into his pocket. "We should get going."

Arnoldo took the bag of weed from his pocket and began re-stuffing his pipe. "If you find it, let me know. I'm going to build a five-star hotel out there. Water is essential."

His words immediately soured Lucy's fun, and she immediately sobered up. "I don't think my pool would like that." She frowned.

"My island, my pool, Lucy," Arnoldo said, and relit his pipe.

Lucy pouted; all the laughter gone.

Freddy grabbed a gallon jug of water and two cans of peanuts, and Lucy added another chocolate candy bar to the goods to buy. They paid and put the items in their day packs. Freddy insisted on carrying the water because he was a man. Lucy once again thought that if Freddy wanted to think that way, it was fine by her.

When they walked out the door, Lucy popped open her umbrella, which made her chuckle. Realizing it wasn't particularly funny, she stopped laughing. They both said goodbye to Fabio, who bobbed his head up and down. He then let out a long moaning sigh and crooned, "I'll pluck you naked."

"That's not nice," Lucy said.

"Sounds like Liam's voice. I wonder when he talked to the bird?" Freddy inquired.

"Harry and Eleanor sitting in a tree..." Fabio sang.

"Odd. Has Eleanor been talking to the bird too?" Freddy readjusted the water and grunted while he shifted the gallon of water to rest on a nonexistent hip, first one, then the other, neither comfortable, then shifted it to the front again, holding it with two hands against his stomach.

"I definitely got a contact high," Lucy said, the umbrella shading her as she stared at the dock.

"Juanita and Bob are reeling in a fish? I'd like some fried fish right now." She took a bag of chips out and slowly ate a few. Bob and Juanita had a hold of the rod and were walking backward.

"Humph," Freddy said. "I don't see Eleanor. I still say underwear. A Greek would swim in their underwear."

"Not if they're modest."

They walked down the main road past the church. The children were now sitting in their seats at their outside desks, neatly lined in rows that created a square. They were reciting the alphabet in English. The teacher was a thin woman with a wrap on her head and a stick in her hand. "I wonder why it's not in Spanish?" Freddy said.

"Most people speak Garifuna or is it Creole? Whatever it is, I think it's more like English."

"I certainly can't understand it."

Lucy and Freddy walked past the church. When they came to the road that led to the dive shop, they noticed fresh tread marks in the mud, thin and wide.

"Someone's been out and about this morning," Freddy remarked.

As they continued on their way, Freddy began to breathe heavier. He shifted the gallon jug around again and again, then stopped to wipe the sweat from his hands.

"Why don't you walk with the water on top of your head?" Lucy suggested.

Making a fish mouth, he said, "Like the women, here. Are you trying to be funny?"

"No."

His perplexed round face swallowed his eyes. When he put the gallon of water on top of his head, his eyes grew big again. As time went on, Lucy offered to carry the water on her head, suggesting they should take turns, and Freddy let her. When they reached the dive shop, they saw the boat was gone and no one was around. "They go out early," Lucy muttered and put the water down on the ground. Famished, they sat on a boulder and ate all the oranges. The surf quiet, the solitude peaceful, they stared off at the shimmering ocean. "Josey says the ocean is like an alluring poem, languid and mysterious," Lucy said.

"I think you have a crush on him," Freddy stated. Not waiting for an answer, he jumped up. "Let's get going."

A few minutes later, they were deep inside the jungle. The tread marks were still very prominent and occasionally made them stumble. The morning air, cooler in the woods, gave them a reprieve from what they felt would be an excruciatingly sultry, hot day.

They carried the water in their arms while looking at the ground for fer-de-lances. If they saw one, they thought they might drop the water on it. They also discovered two forked sticks, which at first, they thought were snakes. Their mutual scare had briefly turned a growing, insufferable hot walk icy. But they got over it by laughing. Their new sticks gave them a sense of professionalism as they felt they had found the perfect tool for their trade.

It was also decided that looking for a lost water source could be considered work.

When Freddy stopped to rub his chin, he saw a bush frosted with little cone-shaped flowers and bees. "That's honeysuckle." He went over, put the water on the ground, picked a flower, and sucked on the end of it. "Very sweet. Come try one."

Lucy joined him. They both stood there for a while sucking the ends of the flowers. When the sun shifted, it brought beams of light into the forest; it was like a spotlight had been directed at them. They wiped their brows and continued on their way.

Once at the beach, they noticed the swells in the ocean were fiercer than the day before. They watched the waves bash the lava rocks with foamy white froth. It was mesmerizing with the grebes swooping across the sun and the driblets of spray splattering the hazy blue background. Lucy licked the salt off her lips and said loudly, because the ocean's roar was deafening, "I could live here!" Then took it back. "If there were a house and a restaurant."

"Give it time," Freddy said.

They looked at each other.

"Such a shame," Lucy mumbled.

And because the beach had gone wild with wind and waves, they couldn't figure out where their tidal pool had gone to. They walked up toward the hill and stood on the periphery of the beach. Freddy took a drink from the water, and so did Lucy. They bounced their eyes over the lava rock, then Lucy pointed with her chin. "There. It's over there." But the pool didn't seem right. There appeared to be an upright log swishing back and forth in it.

"A piece of driftwood," Freddy said and scratched his stubble.

Chapter
18

Paradise Ruined

They walked toward what they thought was a large piece of drift-wood in their pool. The closer they got, the more peculiar the shape of the wood became; it resembled a head on a pair of shoulders, shaggy with seaweed. Lucy put her hand on Freddy to stop. "Do you see what I see?"

"I think it's an illusion. Wood is like that, you know." Freddy made an *O* mouth.

She put her hand on Freddy to stop walking, a look of panic across her face. She handed him the water jug. Freddy took it. Still thirsty, he popped the top off and drank, while Lucy made her way to the pool.

Assessing what she presumed to be the front side of the wood, Lucy walked around to the other side of the pool, her back to the ocean. She gasped, then let out a gut-wrenching, high-pitched shriek.

She'd never made a noise so fierce and animalistic before. It made her dizzy as though the lights went out in her head. It also felt levitating, as though blood stuck in her veins had begun to flow fluidly up into the sky. Refocusing, she screamed again, and twice more, then had to squat down, exhausted.

Freddy put the jug down and ran over to see what was wrong. "What is it! What is it!" he yelled. When he arrived at the pool, his eyes pinned to the driftwood, he yelped a warble sound as though a feather were stuck in his throat. The odd sound made Lucy briefly smile and forget what she had just seen, but then she remembered and felt horribly sick. Freddy stared at the wood and gasped, reeled backward, stumbling over the lumpy terrain, and tumbled onto his butt. Lucy gained some sort of sense, stepped back too from the water's edge, and tripped over Freddy but grabbed his hair to stop herself from falling. She then sat down beside him. Freddy rubbed his head and pinched her.

"Ouch! Why did you do that?"

"You pulled my hair."

"Sorry."

They sat for a moment; neither one had ever seen a dead body before. Finally, Lucy said, "Liam. It's Liam, isn't it?" her voice breathy and dry. "I think I'm going to..." She threw up water and orange bits all over the porous rocks; the water disappeared through the porous lava, and the chunks of fruit were left dappled over the ground. Mouth open, hair flying in the wind, she said, with a slight whimper, "I'll never get that image out of my head."

"Gosh, that's gruesome." Freddy was fixated on her throw-up.

"Maybe our minds just made it up. Maybe that's not really a dead body but driftwood. But what's that stench?" Lucy said, holding her stomach with one hand, her other over her mouth and nose.

"Probably your throw-up," Freddy said, then pausing to sniff the air, he added. "Oh, it's the wind. The wind smells like a dead body. Disgusting." He made a face by bunching his lips over his teeth and held his breath, only to gasp, "Well, he's dead all right. Our minds are not making this up because I know for a fact there is a glaucomic, blue-eyed, bloated dead person who looks like Liam in our pool." Freddy cringed. "The pasty skin, white like rubber. I believe I saw a crab crawl out of his mouth."

"Let's check again," Lucy said and stood up.

They went back over to the pool. The water was clear, and they could see down to his feet. He was shoeless. Small fish were basking in the abundance of meat, nibbling and pulling off chunks; the toes were black, and a few were missing. The tips of his fingers, blue, were attached to white hands that drifted across the top of the water like soft distorted rakes. Most of his body was below the surface of the water, magnified and ghostly white; the small hairs on his arms lined with bubbles made him look like he had goosebumps. The body swayed in the wind like an untethered blow-up doll. His cheeks were concave, like he was sucking on a sour lozenge. Lucy and Freddy spied a dent in the side of his head to the right, which they analyzed as a blow to his cranium. "Murdered," Freddy muttered.

"He had on the same clothing at the bar last night," Lucy added. "Jams and a green short-sleeve polo. Yes, murdered after he left us."

"I've never seen a dead person before," Freddy said. "What a terrible sight."

"Paradise ruined," Lucy mumbled.

"I'm not feeling very happy-go-lucky now. More like unlucky."

"I can't move away. Freddy, take my hand and pull me away."

Just then, a large wave rolled in, bouncing Liam's body into the air. His right arm flew out, slapping his cold, clammy hands onto Lucy's and Freddy's bare legs. They both screamed, a short gargled, glottal stop, and jumped back, tripping over each other's feet; they ran toward the woods. When they stopped and looked back, they saw that the body had turned around and was looking at them, hands out of the water, elbows leaning out, as though wanting to have a conversation.

"Gosh, it's like he's alive," Freddy murmured.

"This is going to give me nightmares." Lucy shrugged and walked away.

"We should report this." Freddy's words stopped her.

Turning to face him, Lucy said, "I've never seen a cop here."

"Maybe the self-imposed mayor?"

"Arnoldo?" Lucy chuckled. It felt good to find humor in such a hideous situation. She walked over to the rocks by the tree line. Wanting to think about their next move, she let her eyes train around for something to sit on. Noticing a cluster of thick hunter-green leaves curled into the shape of a canoe attached to a mangled tree, she walked over. Underneath the tree were small purple fruits that littered the ground. Clustered along the branches of the tree was more of the same fruit. It had to be a mangosteen tree, she thought. She made a little joyful jump and picked one of the fruits and smelled it. Sweet and aromatic with the essence of strawberries, oranges, and pineapples. The wonderful aroma helped cleanse her senses of Liam's dead body, and she was somewhat rejuvenated. Finding herself hungry, she peeled the skin back and took a tiny bite. "Delicious," she mumbled, glad to get the taste of bile out of her mouth. Lucy proceeded to pick several more until a pile grew on the ground in the shape of a haphazard pyramid.

"Freddy!" she shouted and glanced around for him. He was walking toward her with the water jug in his hands. He stopped and glanced up at her. Lucy waved one of the fruits at him. "It's a mangosteen. Fabio will love it."

"I'd like one. All this grotesque death has made me hungry."

She threw one to him and stuffed the rest of the fruit pyramid into her daypack. Freddy stood by her. "Tasty. We should get going, though. We have a crime to report." He sighed, then continued, "Gosh, I'm sweaty and hot."

Lucy looked over at the ocean. The gnashing spray impeded the horizon, while Liam's body swished back and forth like a metronome. "Horrible. Horrible," she muttered and bent over to zip her bag up. "How do you think it happened?"

"Maybe it's not a murder. He went swimming last night and drowned. The fierce storm bashed his head against the rocks and carried him here." While he spoke, his eyes were glued to Liam's swaying body. "He looks like he's having fun."

Then Lucy burst, "Last night. He was chasing—"

"—the Greek. That's right," Freddy said, looking at Lucy. "The bash to the head." Freddy thumped his lower lip with his index finger. "Maybe they fought? She's no timid petal."

"But where would they have fought?" Lucy queried.

"Don't know. Must have been by the water. Yes, that's it. They fought and she karate-chopped his head and threw him in the ocean."

"Folder. It was over the folder." Lucy took a mangosteen out of her bag and peeled it. She broke a chunk off for Freddy, and he popped it into his mouth while she chewed on the other half. They stood in silence looking down the beach away from death. They both gave a big sigh and refocused on Liam. Then in unison, they shivered. "Let's go," Lucy said. They headed off toward the road.

Once deep into the woods, Lucy, who had been lost in thought over their murder case, said, "I bet she did kill him."

"Eleanor? Well, I don't know. Let's think some more about this." Freddy then stopped and peered down at the road. "Why so many tread marks when it rained last night? Why, I believe," he said, bending in toward Lucy, "possibly the mayor is involved, and the Aussies. These tracks look like a jeep and a dirt bike made them."

Lucy sucked in air and held it for a moment, then breathed. "If the mayor's involved, this could get tricky." She took a swig from the gallon of water and smiled. "Why, of course." Then grabbed Freddy's shirttails, her excitement palatable. "You know what we are now? We're happy-go-lucky-dowsing-detectives."

"I've never had so many jobs all at once. Seems tiring."

"You'll manage." Lucy's mind buzzed.

For a few more moments, they again walked in silence. The air smelled like rot and earth and felt like a soggy dish towel. When their sneakers became clumped with a layer of mud, it caused them to wobble, and they stopped kicking it off.

"Who do we tell if the mayor is a suspect? And the Aussies?"

Freddy stopped to scrape the bottom of his shoe on a rock.

"That's a tough one."

They continued down the road, minds churning and spitting out the *whos*, *hows*, and *whys* of the crime. Before they knew it, they had stepped out of the shadowed jungle. Low-lying bushes and clusters of three-foot heliconia flowers that resembled red birds on a stick caught their attention. "Driblets of blood," Freddy cooed.

"I used to like those flowers," Lucy commented.

They saw that the dive shop was bustling with students. The group looked like they had just come back. The students were wandering in and out of the main building with gear. The French woman's poodle followed her around at her heels. The Irish had all their gear neatly placed by them on the dock and looked bored. The Italians had their masks on and regulators in their mouths and were goofing around by the shop door. One of them let all the air out of a tank when the other two weren't looking. Mateo, on the dock, beckoned them to hurry up. The minimal waves rocked the pebbles and shells on the beach, which created the sound of sliding gravel. Lucy and Freddy were sticky with salt, sweat, and humidity; clusters of bug bites bubbled behind their knees. They'd been so involved in their whodunit parables, they forgot to apply bug spray. Their hair was matted to their foreheads and stringy—they toyed with the idea of jumping off the dive shop dock. The divers, now congregated by the Parker, made it not feel right. They listened to Mateo give the group a lecture about what to expect with their midmorning dive.

"Maybe we should go ask the group if they know anything about Liam? Somebody must have seen something," Freddy stated.

"If they give us information, what do we do with it?" Lucy sighed, then added. "I wish Josey were here. He'd know what to do."

"The fact that he went fishing is suspect," Freddy barked.

"We don't know if he's fishing or getting supplies or hooky."

"Are you defending him?" Freddy accused.

"No, but then maybe, yes."

Silent and pensive, Lucy and Freddy began to walk again. Their mood, tense. Their next move, unknown.

Chapter
19

The Suspects

Lucy and Freddy meandered along the road until it met up with the island's main drag. They stood, confused about which way to go, as in whether to tell the mayor or the Aussies. The other possibilities would be Lilly or the Beach Lodge owner, Ernesto, and then there was Milly. But the more they spoke about who might have done it, the more it seemed plausible that everyone was a suspect. "Liam may have been bothering Lilly last night, so she and her sisters bashed him with a pot and tossed him off the back of the restaurant into the ocean," Lucy said.

"And Ernesto, troubled by Liam's drinking, could have knocked him over the head with...with one of his plastic chairs. And dragged him into the sea," Freddy added. "But no matter what, the bike tracks and the jeep ruts make it more likely that the homicidal candidates are the Aussies or Arnoldo or both."

Betting On Paradise

"Motive?"

"Can't think of one. I would like to know what it is, though."

"I don't think anyone liked him. I mean, I suppose he wasn't bad. Just sloppy," Lucy stated.

"Nothing wrong with sloppy." Freddy frowned.

Lucy shrugged. "Such a shame. He wanted to be a poet."

"What he needed was a good Alcoholics Anonymous program. And...a slap in the face. Too late now," Freddy said, scratching his head. "Oh, Josey is a suspect too. Even if you don't like it." He darted his sight toward Lucy and waited for a response. Lucy looked into Freddy's pale blue eyes. She thought of creatures that lived in the dark but could see; only Freddy was the blind one that somehow ate everyone's food when they weren't looking. She wasn't sure why she thought this; she just did.

"Gosh, I'm hungry," Freddy said. He was staring down the road toward the store. "I'd like something other than the peanuts and cookies that I have in this sack, and our water is almost gone. Let's go to the store. We need to tell someone. Why not Arnoldo?"

"Good idea. If he has a strange expression on his face, he probably did it." Lucy's tone was stern.

Heading toward the store, they saw that the school was still in session and that Juanita and Bob had joined the class. Juanita was sitting at a desk listening intently to the teacher read a book. All the other students were quiet too, hands folded, chins straight, feet tucked under. Bob was standing beside Juanita, eyes bearing down on the storyline. An Aesop's fable was being read. The main character, a donkey.

Once at the store, Lucy and Freddy discovered the door locked. Fabio was outside in his cage gazing off at the bay. "Where did Arnoldo go?" Lucy asked Fabio. He answered with a fart noise. Lucy and Freddy laughed. "I guess he doesn't want to say. Strange no one is around."

"Very suspect," Freddy remarked.

Lucy then gave Fabio an unpeeled mangosteen. He took it with a claw and began to peel it with his beak. As he munched on it, he made slushy noises, swallowed, and sang, "I'm in heaven..." Lucy tossed several more into the cage and kept the rest for training purposes.

They then walked around to the backside of the store and checked the rear door. It was locked, too. Stumped, they stood a moment in silence to think. Chickens clucked and nibbled at the ground by a table, while a light dusty breeze mussed up their dripping sweat.

"This is sooo...weird. Since being here, the store is always open during the day," Freddy said.

"Now what?" Lucy queried and fanned herself with her hand.

"Lunch."

Milly was bent over, elbows on the counter of her gin bar. She watched them walk over and sit down on two stools across from her. Milly's smooth dark brown cheeks were glistening in the heat. Voices echoing up the hill from the dock caused her to redirect her attention to the bay. Lucy and Freddy followed her gaze, which went to the mailboat. The sounds seemed to be coming from Eleanor and Juan. Eleanor was sitting on a low beach chair at the end of the dock sunning, her legs stretched out. She had a round-brimmed straw hat on her head as big as an umbrella. Juan was standing at the back of the boat, fishing. They were talking to each other, but due to the distance, the words were muffled and incoherent.

"The engine's broke," Milly said. She stood upright and refocused her attention on Lucy and Freddy. "What can I get you?"

"Lunch," Freddy said again, only this time as a directive.

"A little early, but I can put something together. Grouper, beans, coconut rice. To drink?" Her brown eyes had a hint of green and heralded a knowing intelligence that Lucy believed came from running a business with a clientele that spoke of the outside world. It made her want to have a business too, but she had no idea what kind; a jewelry shop came to mind, along with a fashionable scarf boutique. As she watched Milly's every move—the quizzical turn of the head, the arch of the brow, the manner in which she stood: shoulders back, breast out, buttocks ample and able—Lucy sensed an abundance of confidence in Milly's presence. *Possibly an old soul*, she thought. As for herself, she hadn't ripened yet, she pouted, although she was fine with it. *Who knows what I will become?* It made her smile to think she could be anything and anybody. Presently, she was stuck on being Italian and a happy-go-lucky-dowser/detective, but that could change at the drop of a hat. Liam was a drunk and now he was dead; life was fickle and unpredictable. He had wanted to be a poet, an artist. What a shame to die before one was finished. Then she recoiled in her seat as death, with its bloodless, white, and vacant eyes, flooded her thoughts. She tapped her head hard with an index finger to knock the ghastly images away.

Milly, who stood patiently waiting for their drink order, took hold of Lucy's hand and said, "My dear, what on earth are you doing?" Then gave her hand back, but let her eyes linger a while upon Lucy's troubled face with concern.

It felt comforting to have Milly hold her hand but also not right. She knew she was acting odd and glanced at Freddy, who said, "We've had a rough morning."

"I'd like a gin and tonic. Light on the tonic," Lucy said.

Milly smiled. "Two."

"Yup," Freddy remarked.

They watched her make their drinks. Her hair tied up and wrapped in a bright lemony scarf complemented her cotton salmon shift. Unlike a language, a body color and shape could not be faked. Milly's full lips were like pieces of a peach. Although Lucy couldn't be Milly, she could be like her. She would buy a colorful headscarf and a lovely colored dress. She would not just be a Spanish/English-speaking Italian but a fashionable one too and said, "*Theha luncha speciales sounda gooda, toa.*"

Freddy snapped his head around and looked at her. "One day the men in white are going to wrap you into a pretzel and take you away."

"I suppose. But they don't exist here, so it doesn't matter," Lucy remarked with her very own American accent.

Milly laughed like a bellowing bass drum submerged in water. She stopped to place their drinks in front of them and chuckled. "You two are starting early."

"As Freddy said, we've had a rough morning." Lucy dug into her day pack for the baggie of stogies and matches. "We found a dead guy." She lit her cigar and puffed on it several times before removing it from her mouth.

Freddy gasped. "Lucy, I thought we were telling Arnoldo first." Then to Milly: "We've come up with a lot of suspects. You're not one, yet."

"A dead body, where?" Milly's eyes tightened.

"Squash Beach. In our..." Lucy looked at Freddy with sad eyes. "...

pool." Lucy offered Freddy and Milly a cigar. They each took one. Milly lit the finger-size smokes with her lighter. All three tugged, puffed, and stared off toward the bay. Finally, Milly broke the silence. "Shot?" she questioned and let out a pristine line of smoke.

"Didn't look like it," Freddy answered, as though an expert on the subject. "Nothing like an autopsy."

Milly laughed, again a base drum but this time hitting a wild note. "Ha-ha... Occasionally a dead body lands on these shores. We let the birds take care of them. God giveth and taketh. Amen. Now, excuse me. I am goin' to cook you two up some lunch."

She sashayed into the kitchen. Freddy leaned into Lucy. "Do you think she did it? Very cavalier."

Lucy thought over the word *cavalier*, and once again wondered why Freddy, whose native tongue was Danish, had such a good vocabulary. "Maybe," she said, then sighed. "But why would she?"

"I am sure he racked up quite a bill here. They fought over his debt. Milly throttled him and snapped his neck by accident. She's a big girl. Strong."

"Yes, yes. Possibly."

They sipped their drinks and stared at Milly by the fryolator. She stepped away from their sight. Beads of sweat and flies caused them to dab their foreheads and slap the air. When a low voice could be heard from the kitchen, Lucy shouted, "Milly! Are you talking to us?" Milly stepped back into view with a radio receiver in her left hand. "No," she remarked poking her head around the door to look at them, then stepped away again.

"Are you talking to someone on the radio?" Lucy questioned.

"Very, very suspect. Who do you think she called?" Freddy whispered.

"Strange."

As asked for, there was more gin than tonic; the booze swam into their heads and stayed. Hearing commotion from the dock, they both glanced over at the mail boat. They saw Juan had fallen asleep on a bench, his fishing rod against the gunwale. Eleanor had gotten out of her chair that was on the dock. They watched her toss it into the boat, along with her hat and some other items, then step back and gaze over the bay. A moment passed, and she picked up a small knapsack by her feet and began to walk down the dock toward the land. Her saunter was casual, and her hair was in a ponytail, which wagged like a dog's tail with each step.

"Where do you think she's going?" Freddy inquired. His drink half gone, he emptied the rest with one large gulp.

"If she killed him, she must be one of those psychotics who find killing like eating ice cream. Look how happy she is," Lucy remarked, enmeshed in analyzing Eleanor. She continued, "Her dark sunglasses, loose shorts, and billowing white shirt; her walk; the swing of her arms. I can't make out her face, but I think she's smiling." She then huffed, took a glorious puff off her stogie, and exhaled a blue cloud of smoke that circled her head in hypnotic spirals, and added, "If she didn't kill him, well, I think she might be like us, a happy-go-lucky."

"Happy-go-lucky and murder are like oil and water." He sucked the last tidbits of gin from the ice and then began to crunch the frozen bits. "I'm merely a dowsing-detective now. And that woman? Why, she's a suspected cold-blooded murderer. Nothing more, nothing less." He then stared at his empty glass, shrugged, and looked over at the backside of Milly at the stove. "She's cooking now. Very, very suspect that call she made," then shouted, "Milly, since you're busy, can I make myself another drink?"

"Help yahself."

"He made the drinks eight-count gin, a splash of tonic, and a squeeze of lime. He made another for Lucy too since she was down to only ice. When he sat back down at his seat, he lifted his drink into the air and declared, "To being distraught and disgusted by mankind."

"To living life to its fullest!" Lucy shouted. The gin had lifted her mood. She picked up her freshened beverage and licked the rim. "Very tasty, Freddy."

"I bet I'll never be happy again." Freddy frowned.

"I bet you will."

They shook.

In the distance, weaving in between the languid wafts of warm air and frying fish came the *waaa...braap* whine of a dirt bike engine. It was Arnoldo. His body curled, his elbows up, and sunglasses dipped on his nose, he sped around the bend by the houses, nearly hitting Eleanor. She jumped out of the way. Unfazed by his near roadkill, Arnoldo roared up to the church. Students were sitting in their seats coloring. Juanita was showing Bob her artwork. Arnoldo stormed over, grabbed Bob's collar, and began dragging him away. Juanita got up and held on to Bob's rump to keep him from being taken. The tug-of-war ended when the teacher came over. A discussion ensued. Whatever words passed, Bob was allowed to stay. Arnoldo got back on his bike and zoomed off, away from the church and the store. He took a turn toward the leeward side of the island. The shifts and grinds of gears faded into the distance.

Milly walked in and placed fish, beans, and rice on mustard-colored ceramic plates in front of Lucy and Freddy. She had been watching Arnoldo, too, and shook her head. "My...my, that man is too much sometimes."

Another engine sound caught their attention. It was Dan in a topless white jeep. He was speeding down the main drag and took a sharp right toward the dive shop, too, his usually wet, matted hair flying in the breeze.

"I think they're going to Squash Beach," Lucy said and dug into her food.

"Very suspect," Freddy added and took a large gulp of his drink.

Milly chortled. "Hell, those boys? Scouting out the best location for the five-star hotel. They go every day."

Lucy and Freddy gave each other a telepathic glance. Lucy leaned into Freddy and loudly whispered, "She knows something."

"Very suspect," Freddy said and eyeballed Milly.

"Now you two, hush." Her rich, plump mouth was open. She chided them with her index finger. "A bunch of petulant busybodies. That man in yah pool could be off a cruise ship. Happens. Wife could have pushed him. No point in getting the woman in trouble. No doubt a cheater."

Freddy, with a mouthful of fish and rice, swallowed, "But it's Liam. The new guy. Lucy identified the body."

"Liam. Who's Liam?" Milly's left brow danced.

"The new guy. Lucy identified him. You see, she liked to stare at him," Freddy explained. "Knows what he looks like. I know what he

174

looks like, too. Not a lot of Liam types around here. Only one. He's dead."

"I don't know why I stare. I guess it's something I do." Lucy took a sip of her drink; she wanted to work on not staring anymore because it was childish.

Milly placed her elbows on the counter, her head level with theirs. "Oh, that guy. Well, now, you two listen—unnatural deaths and murders aren't good for business."

"What makes you think it was unnatural?" Freddy questioned, a smug expression on his face. He added, "Gosh, I think I do make a good detective."

Milly shrugged as though his statement was juvenile and went into the kitchen to clean up.

"His family should be informed," Lucy shouted at Milly's back.

Milly walked back into the bar area with a huff. "You two, finish your food and gins. Go take a nap." Her tone was firm and riddled with annoyance. "Come back in the late afternoon. Arnoldo, you, me—we'll all go to Squash Beach and see about this dead fellow."

"You're all *suuuspects*," Freddy barked; his words had begun to slur.

"Good God, give me strength. In this country, the people who discover the body are thought to be the killers. Therefore, you two are the main suspects." Milly's tone was gruff.

"*Thaaat's* not right." Lucy balked, her speech was troubled too. She put her drink down hard on the counter, then thought otherwise and chugged several more gulps until it was all gone.

"*Billth, blease,*" Freddy said to Milly, then rounded toward Lucy. "We need to sober up." He finished the rest of his drink and stuffed several spoonfuls of food into his mouth, then added, with bits of rice falling off his lips, "Lucy, eat *domething.* We might have to defend ourselves *yater.*"

Lucy puffed on her cigar and ignored her food. She reached into her bag for a clump of Lempiras and put them on the counter. "Liam was my *briend*, and I am very saddened by his *heath.*"

"Whaa..." Freddy said, staring at her. Uncertain about her line of thought, he fiddled with his shirtsleeves, then made an *O* mouth as though understanding. "Why. My *briend* too. We're very sad."

"Really? What's his last name?" Milly asked.

"Liam. Liam Liam," Lucy said and got up. Milly's drum laugh went wild again and hit all sorts of peculiar notes. Lucy made an *O* mouth like Freddy as though offended. "I had another *briend* die today too. This morning. His *name* was fly. And guess *phrat* they are both finally doing now? No*ffing.* I'm not ready to completely do *nothing.*"

Freddy, who listened in earnest, sat back and almost fell off his stool. "Lucy, we need *crediblititity.* That fly *briend* of yours. Well. It's just nutty."

"That's very *bhurtful*, Freddy."

He leaned into her and whispered, "You had the right idea of Liam being our *briend*. Now don't go batty and ruin everything. I don't want to go to jail." He tugged Lucy off her chair and dragged her away. "We'll be back," he shouted at Milly. "You see, we're mere *bowsers* looking for water and came across a dead body, which made us detective-*bowsers*, but now I'm going back to just being a *bowser*. In a court of law, your system won't hold up, and our duty as dowsers will, along with being good Samaritans." Freddy paused here because he forgot what else he wanted to say, so Lucy filled in: "He's in our pool. We want him removed." Finding it hard to stand still, she steadied herself by putting a hand on Freddy's shoulder. "You're very manly, Freddy." She began to poke his shoulder to feel his muscles.

"Stop that." He removed her hand.

Lucy looked at Milly. "Yes, he's our good *briend* Liam. We're happy to have him in our pool, but we also need him out."

Huffing, Freddy took hold of Lucy's day pack that was on her back and pulled her toward the road. They teetered off with Freddy bemoaning the unfair system of "guilty, until proven innocent." When it finally sunk in, that her freedom may end, Lucy let out a wail. Behind them, they could feel and hear Milly shrug with light laughter. "I don't *dink* we handled this well," Freddy said, and Lucy added, "I *dink* you're right. As they walked, they began to recount documentaries and movies that described the foul conditions of foreign prisons: no real toilets; watery, rotten food; abuses of a hellacious nature; putrescent lice crawling in bedding; no ability to prove their innocence, as they were each other's alibi. By the time they reached the beach lodge, their doom and gloom for themselves had somehow shifted. Lucy, unable to contend with life in prison, especially a foreign prison shouted into the air, "For *Frist's* sakes, who kills a *briend*? Oh, Freddy, let's not think about the cruelties of humanity anymore." And like a light switch turning a dark room bright, they stopped thinking about prison to celebrate their "good friend" Liam's life.

"So very young and a..a..I guess an artist. But not very well liked," Freddy groused.

"Handsome but old. My parents' age. Or maybe older. No, just old," Lucy lamented.

"Such a waste," Freddy ballyhooed.

"Such a nice smile," Lucy caterwauled.

Once on the beach, they tossed off their clothes. They had their bathing suits underneath and swam. But not too deep, as they didn't want to end up like their "good friend" Liam.

"To Liam's new home. The ocean," Freddy shouted.

"Cheers to beers and legs behind your ears," Lucy followed up.

"Life is a waste of time, and time is a waste of life. So, let's get wasted all of the time and have the time of our life," Freddy said and kicked the water with his feet.

"That's a good one, Freddy. Ha...ha...I wish I had a drink," Lucy said. Pretending to have a glass in her hand she burst, "Cheers to Liam and big-breasted women!" She looked down at her breasts. "I'm not one of them, but, well..."

"I like your breasts," Freddy said and stood up in the water to look at Lucy.

"You've never seen them."

"If I saw them, I believe they would be nice."

"Odd," Lucy said, not sure if she liked where the conversation was going. Changing the subject, she suggested, "Let's build a memorial for Liam." They got out of the water and searched the shore for rocks. They found several large and small and piled them into a pyramid. Exhausted from so much exertion and drink, they found a patch of hot sand under a cluster of palm trees, threw their towels down, and tumbled on top of them. Lying on their backs, they stared up into the sky with heavy, sleepy eyes, but before falling asleep, Lucy asked, "Are you happy again, Freddy?"

"Why, yes, I am."

"You owe me a pilito."

Chapter
20

The Folder

The front door to the Beach Lodge was open. The only signs of Ernesto: a shapeless, plastic chair by the entrance and a dirty plate with specks of food and flies on it. Eleanor walked into the dim, unlit hall. It smelled of cleaning fluids. At the other end was a bright beacon of light alluding to a beach, a blinding plethora of pastel blues, cream-colored sand, and speckles of blushing clouds. It gave one the impression they were walking toward Shangri-la.

Eleanor's thoughts were concentrated on the vortex of swimming, relaxing, and reading. It was a beautiful sunny day. She wanted to listen to the waves roll onto the sand and not Juan's fitful snoring while he fished. At the end of the hallway, she stopped to take in the sunlight that came in from a window above the back stairwell. It zigzagged like a modern painting as it created white stripes that shimmered uniformly on the walls. The steps were caramel-colored wood. A house fly buzzed by leaving silence behind. In the distance, soft rumbles of the ocean could be heard. It was as though the hoopla and chaos of the world no longer existed in this lodge. It also reminded her of being a child—summers on Cape Cod as a youngster at her grandparents' house. There had been dunes in their front yard. The lazy summer sun wrang clapboards dry. A sense of being safe and cared for, a hug, a bellow of laughter. And yet, as lovely as it all had been, the memories made her sad. *Could life ever be as blissful, again?* she thought with a hint of hope. She took a deep breath in through her nose and let the air out slowly through her mouth. Then she smiled. "A room here would be nice." She walked outside.

A hammock was tied between two palm trees to her right, and she went over to it. Large and made of grayish cotton rope, hammocks were not her favorite bed—too flimsy and unstable. But for lying on a beach while reading a book or taking a nap, they possessed a pleasant, languid vibe. She put her towel over it for comfort and sat, then swung her legs up. It had a solid feel to it, and she wiggled into a comfortable position. With her feet a foot off the ground, she put a foot in the sand and pushed herself to and fro. A couple of black birds with red on their beaks were in the palm trees above. They warbled at each other with long tunes and short shrills. The breeze, nothing but a baby's sigh, was sweet and aromatic. "Perfect," she said to the sky. Then she cringed. *Last night was a nightmare—today the world has become heaven on earth, at least for the time being.*

She took a book out of her satchel and opened it. It was a trashy romance novel in Spanish, another item she had gotten from Juan's mother. Although the writing was simple and racy, the effort it took to concentrate on the book wasn't there. She placed the novella on her belly and reached down into her bag for the folder she had taken from Liam the day before. Opening it, she stared at the photos. She dismissed the pictures of Yena and the boy, to concentrate on Harry's. Barely a man when the photo was taken—his cheeks rounder, his hair shorter, his body lighter—one could see the beginnings of his more angled, beautiful face. The desire to see him in person again gripped her with a small ache to her heart. She glanced up to look at the black birds. "Do you know where Harry might be?" She leveled her eyes toward the ocean and spoke again: "Harry, why did Liam come here looking for you? Did you plant a decoy? Sounds like you." She glanced at his photo again. *I think you're in Europe. Buying up property and selling it for a profit? Or teaching?* She was sure he was using an alias. *One with distinction and promise. And most likely in love with an exotic woman. Someone impressively talented and sensual.* "Are you in love again, Harry?" she whispered. She didn't bother to inquire whether he might be thinking of her since their relationship had been short. And his life, so preoccupied with the pitter-patter game of cat and mouse. Although she missed him, Eleanor did find the downplaying of their romance a helpful ploy to digest that it was over.

She rocked to and fro with a lazy sigh. It was not as though she knew him well either, she thought. A few months of sex, drinking, and playing cards didn't count for much, except a good time. Eleanor tucked the pictures behind a three-page report and began to read the document.

Everything that Liam had spoken about was there: *Harry's parents and their business ties with Liam's family (the Ramos's), who also appeared to have ties with the Pinochet government. Or at least the report hinted at it because the document alluded to President Pinochet being upset over the wrongdoing. Pinochet backed the Ramos's by giving them full police and military support to find the criminals (Unias). The exact amount stolen was in the millions and included real estate and jewelry; noted was a gold watch that had been given to Umberto Ramos by the King of Spain.*

Senior Umberto Ramos and his wife, Flora, had filed charges against the Unias family in 1981. Eleanor paused to think how old Harry was then. If she had Harry's age correct, he would have been twenty-four or -five, she thought, then continued reading. *His parents and sister were arrested on January 5, 1981. After several months in jail, Don Ricardo Unias confessed to stealing the Ramos's money, property, and jewel-*

ry. Problems arose when Umberto Ramos went to retrieve the stolen goods; there was nothing to take. The Unias family had very little money in their bank account, and the only property they owned was their house in Santiago, Chile. Ricardo Unias, his wife, Julieta, and their daughter, Soledad, were killed while trying to escape from jail. It is alleged that the Unias' son, Heraldo, along with his aunt, Yenara Pinola Alvares, have possession of the stolen property.

The report went on to say that Heraldo Unias, the son, had been in England during the arrests of his parents and sister. When they tried to track Heraldo's whereabouts, he was nowhere to be found. Yenara Alvares and two boys (one recently murdered) and the brother (who recently died of consumption) had fled in the winter of 1981, after the raid on the family. They managed to get out of the country and move to El Puente, Guatemala. The fugitives bought land and prospered for many years. Heraldo joined them. He worked at an orphanage nearby to ward off suspicions, along with using the name Harry Van Cleef. His reason for being in the area was to help his aunt Yenara sell off the investments they'd made with the stolen money in Guatemala (laundered monies). When land prices rose due to oil prospects, they sold it all, making a hefty profit. All was going well for them until a man named Daniel Scotchwick showed up and kidnapped the fifteen-year-old nephew of Alvares. Scotchwick wanted money for the child after finding out the family was rich. How he found this out is still unknown. Scotchwick was given the amount of money he asked for (which is also unknown) but still ended up killing the boy. Heraldo became acquaintances with Scotchwick. It is thought that this friendship arose in order that Heraldo could find out what happened and seek revenge. Scotchwick ended up being murdered in June 1991. Heraldo Unias is now wanted for this murder although it is noted he did not commit the homicide but ordered it and that a prominent wealthy sesame farmer named Rubin Sanchez and his partner Enrique Vasques are the killers of Dan Scotchwick. It is still unknown why Sanchez or Vasquez would do such a thing since they didn't need the money. It wasn't long after the death of Scotchwick that the fugitives had been identified by Dori Ramos, who was going by the name Titlemen. He was vacationing at the Club de Bote across from the orphan-

age, where Heraldo (aka Harry Van Cleef) was living. The police raid on the fugitives in El Puente and the orphanage was foiled by someone tipping off Yenara Alvares and Heraldo Unias (aka, Harry Van Cleef) at the last minute. Hence, they were able to escape.

Eleanor placed the folder on her chest. It was clear as day now, written in ink, Dori and Liam were brothers. How awful. She remembered that fateful night at the wealthy yachting club, across the river from the orphanage.

The owners had thrown a party for all the volunteers. Vasques and Sanchez had been there. They had asked her to go fishing with them. To think they are the ones that took out Scotchwick? She wasn't upset that he had been murdered. Scotchwick had an evilness to him that appeared inborn. She also recalled, several weeks after the party, the evening Harry left and never came back again. She had been ill from an abundance of fire ant bites and an allergic reaction to them. His abandonment added to her fever. In the end, all was fine, and she recovered from her anaphylactic reaction to the bites. When the police found a dead body in the river, everyone thought it was Harry. When she found out it wasn't his but Scotchwick's, she forgave Harry for leaving her so abruptly. She knew he had no other choice. She did find it odd that this man, Harry Van Cleef (Heraldo), had tumbled back into her life—she also felt a sick hollowness in her stomach. Dorian Titlemen, who she had left the orphanage with and sailed around Belize for a month with, was Dori Ramos. Bile crept into her throat. She swallowed, took a sip of water, and stared up at the birds. "How fucked up," she mumbled. Two birds looked down at her, and she smiled at them. "How could this have happened?" Although she wasn't sure who the criminals were. It was a toss-up. Did Harry and his aunt steal the Ramos'money, or did the Ramos's just want all the money for themselves and trumped up a scheme to get it? She finished reading the last sentence of the report: *It has been discovered that Heraldo Unias and Yenara Alvarez, having sold all their real estate investments in Guatemala, are now residing in Honduras.*

She bit a nail and glanced back over the report. *Why would they think they're in Honduras?* She flipped the pages around, convinced she must have missed something. On the back of the last page, written in messy script, there was a note that read: *The Chilean Consulate in Mexico City had been informed by the Minister of Interior of Honduras that Heraldo Unias and Yenara Alvares were seen in Tegucigalpa, Honduras.* Then under the footnote in a different, neater script, it was noted: *A redheaded German named Alex (although drunk) informed my cousin and me (Liam Ramos, aka, Titlemen) that Heraldo Unias is living on the island of Roatan.*

The note was signed and dated, *LT, June 1992.*

"Roatan? Did Alex make that up? Possibly," Eleanor mumbled. She knew Alex from the orphanage and had recently seen him again in La Ceiba. He was an insufferable ass. However, she hoped he had been throwing the men off Harry's trail but then again *Alex was an ass, or was Harry the ass?*

She put the folder back into her bag, stretched, then winced. Her left foot had a purple-blue bruise by her big toe. She flexed her foot to try to stretch the ache away. Her right knuckles were split and red, her wrist swollen, and the skin was split, as it had been rubbed raw by Liam's inflexible grip, and her lower lip was tender from his slap. Touching her tongue to the small cut, Eleanor replayed in her head the night's events.

Chapter
21

Last Night

After arriving back to the boat from the Porch Bar and Grill, Eleanor saw that Juan was hungry and waiting for her. He had set up a small table between the cockpit benches. Bowls, spoons, and beers were placed neatly out. As it was evening and the mosquitoes were feasting too, he had put a citronella candle on the table and another under it. The moon, full and bright, dazzled the bay with white sparkles. The humid air was heavy and laden with a downdraft. Juan mumbled something about a storm brewing. It was hard to see at first, but when they both scanned the horizon, they saw there was a deeper and angry stroke of darkness. A look no boater wanted to see. The boat had also begun to rock more; the light fluffy wind gusted in latent intervals.

"No bread?" Juan asked, sitting down.

"I forgot." It was a lie. She was afraid Liam might have followed her from the Porch Bar and Grill and did not want to have a fight with him alone in the dark by the closed No Name restaurant.

Eleanor put the pot of coconut snapper soup that Aurora had given her on the table and began to ladle out large spoonfuls of the wonderful-smelling soup into their bowls. She felt relieved to be on the boat with Juan, his age and height deceptive. As the saying went, "The man was as strong as an ox" and had a very fatherly, protective manner toward her.

When they both sat down and began to eat, neither one talked at first. It was late evening, and they were exceptionally hungry. What happened next was very sudden and unexpected. A board on the dock creaked, and someone leaped onto the deck of the boat. Eleanor screamed and cursed. She remembered thinking it was a wild animal of some sort.

Then the candle and moon lit the animal's face. It was Liam. For all the excessive drama of his entrance, he was just standing in front of them not doing anything or saying a word. He then huffed, grunted, and looked at Eleanor, then over to Juan, and from Juan to Eleanor as though frisking them with his eyes. His thin, short hair was clumped in places as though he had pulled on it with a hand full of glue. His bangs unfurled; he brushed them back while biting his lip with his front teeth. She figured he was drunk, but then since he was steady on his feet, she wasn't sure.

Eleanor did notice Juan get up and start to inch his way toward the pilothouse door. This caused her to act too. She reached over and grabbed the fishing rod Juan had used earlier without success, hence the soup. Still sitting, she held the rod in front of her like a weapon.

Liam rolled his eyes and laughed like a parent who had lost patience with his child and chided, "Juan, sit back down!" Juan stopped in his tracks but didn't sit. Then Liam looked at both of them and said matter-of-factly, "What's all this? No hugs? Daddy's home for dinner." He laughed again, an airy, light-hearted guffaw and sat down at the table. He picked up a napkin and stuffed it into his shirt front, then gave the table a once-over. "Who spilled the soup? Because in my household, when someone spills the soup, they receive a bottom thrashing." He paused to smile.

"I spilled the beer," Juan said, turning his bottom toward Liam, who made a disgusted expression. He then eyeballed Eleanor and said, "My dear, I believe it was you. Come over so I can give your tush a paddle."

Eleanor didn't move. She recalled wanting to jump overboard or possibly run around him and escape by the dock. Neither idea seemed wrong nor correct to her. She felt stuck, or was it ill? He obviously had followed her back from the Porch Bar and Grill but not immediately. She wondered why. When he placed a half-eaten loaf of pan de coco on the table, the mystery was solved.

"I stopped off at the No Name. Thought you would be there, my dear. Lovely Lilly gave me a loaf of bread on the house. I saved you some. Eat." Liam took out of his pocket a stubby cigar and smelled it. "Smells like fish." He lit it and puffed several times until the end stayed smoking. "Lilly told me to come back for breakfast tomorrow. And if I'm still around on Tuesday, she'll have bacon." He held the baggie of stogies toward Eleanor and then Juan. "Would you like one?"

Nobody said anything.

"Not a talkative group. Well, I'll get to the point. I need my folder. If I don't get my folder back with all the information in it..." He gazed off into the bay and then quickly returned his attention to Eleanor. "...my family will be very, very mad at me. And I can't have that. You see, I'm not equipped to live on my own yet." Sighing, he continued, "Can't afford the lifestyle I'm not only accustomed to but meant to have."

"What folder?" Eleanor responded, eyes tight, her stomach somewhere in her throat—all the signs of a guilty person. *But no*, she thought. *He's drunk, and drunks misplace stuff all the time.* "Whatever you're missing, you probably dropped it in the water, or it blew away. You did pass out on the beach," she snapped.

He leaned back and sniffled. "I don't lose things. I dismiss people, I leave, go, come, stay, climb, hike, walk, read, eat—well, you get the point—but I don't lose things." He glanced quickly at Juan as though to make sure he was still standing there. Refocused on Eleanor, he added, "I had it when I was on this boat. Funny. When I went to read it in my insufferable room at that fly-ridden Beach Lodge, gone." Liam turned toward Juan, again. "Do you have any liquor? I prefer whiskey."

"Only beer," he answered.

"How low. I'll take one." Juan took a beer out of the cooler, opened it, and handed it to him. Liam took a swig and belched. "Anyway, where is it? I want to leave and go get a real drink."

"Maybe you left it in Roatan," Eleanor said. She stood up and leaned against the gunwale. The rod still in her hands, and with her grip tight and slightly shaky, she tried her best to seem nonchalant.

"You know him. Don't you? The expression on your face when you heard his name. A dead giveaway. Even though the Johannesburg authorities decided I had become a liability—stupid idiots—I was one of the best. You see, I'm very good at reading people." He snapped his fingers and said, "Give it here."

Eleanor fiddled with the handle of the fishing rod while keeping her eyes fixated on Liam. His insistence; his snide manner; his spoiled, narcissistic nature, offensive. What also bothered her, he knew she had taken the folder, but he must have doubted himself. "You're a drunk.

How would you know what you did with the folder?" she snapped again, his drunkenness her only line of defense.

An irritated expression crossed Liam's face. Without further warning, he flew out of his seat and lunged at her, knocking the table over. The spoons, plates, and candles hit the floor with a loud, disheveled clatter.

Eleanor swiped at him with the rod. He ducked and she missed. He grabbed her wrist and yanked her toward him. The rod fell from her hand as she winced at his sweaty yet unshakable hold. She pulled away and stumbled into a mailbag, his gripe held as he leaned into her. With his body twisted, the moon shone upon his face, exposing a maniacal, crazed expression; his mouth lined with spittle; his upper lip plastered above his teeth; his focus diffused and detached. With his free hand, he slapped her cheek and mouth. Stunned, she stopped trying to get away for a brief second. The fracas temporarily paused, her hot cheek stung, her temper inflamed, she wasn't going to let him hit her again. She kicked at him and slammed the side of his kneecap with her bare foot. She felt it dislodge. It also hurt her foot. She winced and swore. Liam bent over with a groan and let go of her wrist.

Repulsed by his kneecap pushed to the side and out of its socket, she shrunk back against the bow. But then she thought, *he's bent over and injured, the perfect opportunity to apply the coup d'état.* Eleanor, enlivened by her previous success, went to kick him again. Apparently, he had anticipated her move and bolted up and growled, "Bitch!" His arm drawn back and fist tightened, he was ready to strike her again. She screamed. Then in defense, she punched him as hard as she could in the cheek. He fell sideways and hung over the gunwale. His body tittered, then fell overboard, the splash startling to hear.

Eleanor's hand throbbed, a testament that she had hit him hard, but how could she have ever knocked him out? When a floorboard squeaked, she looked up from the water and Liam, and saw Juan. He stood a few feet from the gunwale. He had a foot-long iron pipe in his right hand, his face pensive. He tossed the pipe into the water and stared at Liam's motionless, floating body. His head knocking into the hull produced the only sound to be heard.

Moments passed. Neither one was able to move away from the side of the boat and the sight of Liam, the incessant knocking gruesome. When Eleanor sighed, Juan looked at her and she at him. She stared at him with wonder. Juan gave a macho shrug. When they looked back down at the body, it was gone. It puzzled them to think the body had sunk within a few seconds. "It's the current," Juan said. "Look how it swirls by the boat now, must be due to the storm coming in." Swells in the bay had grown and the wind had begun to gust sending the boat rocking. Eleanor's breathing grew shallow, the taste of dread tinny and dry. The no return of a deed already done, the wishful thinking the day had never begun.

Yards away, Liam appeared again. His body rolled in the current as the outgoing tide pulled him deeper into the bay. Eleanor thought about the rubber life raft on board. Small, it doubled as a dinghy. But what would be the point in rescuing him? If he were alive, he'd most likely recover and attack her again. If he were dead, which he most likely was, how would they explain his sudden death? Juan's face placid, Eleanor's jumpy, they watched in silence as Liam floated off, his pistachio colored shirt, neon in the moonlight, and then he was gone.

But something else was wrong. When a waft of smoke infused the air, they turned and looked at each other with a different terror. Below them, they could hear the crackle and snap of fire. Juan charged down the ladder to the cabins, Eleanor close behind.

The interior was on fire. A melted citronella candle had puddled on the floor by the open engine door. The flames fluttered yellows and reds. Papers and wood blazed along the floor and the walls. Splinters of ash and sparks flew around the room. A small bang followed by voluminous clouds of sooty smoke knocked them into each other. "The engine may blow," Juan said and grabbed the fire extinguisher, while Eleanor began to swat out the flames on the cabin walls with a sheet from her room. They coughed and sputtered and held their shirts up over their mouths. Finally, they managed to put the fire out, but the damage was done.

The engine wiring was frayed. The hallway was charred and smoldered. The smoke and the heat, nauseating. They walked back up on deck and coughed and spit chunks of black gunk into the water; beads and streams of sweat created rivets on their blackened, sooty bodies. After taking in several lungfuls of clean air, they wiped their brows and mouths with a clean cloth found in the pilothouse. Juan popped the top off two beers and handed one to Eleanor. They sat together on the dock side of the boat to look out over the bay. The beers cooled their scorched throats. When the harrowing realization of having killed a man settled in, their eyes darted toward the row houses. There were none in sight. They were blocked by the other dock and the bend in the bay. A feeling of relief swept over them. "None of those busybody dwellers could have seen a thing," Juan said, glancing up the embankment at the store. The store door was shut, and the lights were off.

"Obviously closed for the night or no one is home."

"The divers and other islanders?" Eleanor questioned.

Juan yawned. "Beach Lodge or the Porch Bar and Grill." The fishing boats in the bay, dark and vacant. Juan brushed his bald head and smiled. "Good," then turned toward Eleanor. "I had images of having a fun night with him but nothing like this."

Eleanor chuckled, more from nerves than his remark being funny. "Thank you, Juan." She knew that he knew that if she hadn't taken the folder, a man would not have been killed and the boat would not be damaged. "I... I..." What does one say when they have created such a mess? Her brain fussed. *Apologize again.* "Juan, I'm so sorry for—"

"—nothing. Nothing happened." He made the gesture of locking his lips with his fingers.

"Your boat?" Guilt clawed at her. The death of Liam, not so much. But how he died, not so great. Being party to a murder, difficult to fathom.

"Boats catch on fire all the time. Bad wiring. Hell, it was meant to be." He sat down on the starboard-side bench and put his feet up to stretch. He then placed his hands on his belly and smiled. "We take a vacation here. I've been needing one, you know. It's a sign from God. He broke my boat so I could rest." He laughed. "I will call my mother—"

"—and your wife."

"Yes, my wife too. All of us, a big vacation. Maybe I'll change jobs. Use this boat for what it is supposed to be. Lobstering." He grinned. "Do you think Arnoldo likes me? You know..."

Eleanor shook her head in disbelief and went over to the cooler. "With all that just happened and you're thinking of Arnoldo, but hey...who knows?" She retrieved two beers, gave Juan one, and sat on the port-side bench with the other. Juan continued to talk and talk, and Eleanor listened. His mood light, his voice dreamy, he spoke about how much fun his mother would have rolling cigars with Lilly and her sisters, and the glory of eating lobster for dinner whenever they felt like it. Eleanor, relieved to see him so lighthearted, shifted her cold bottle from her hand to her lip and back again. Yes, it was as though nothing had happened.

After a few more beers, they both lay back on their respective benches. The stars had disappeared, the air heavy and damp, their minds and bodies zapped of energy. Sleep came fast but was short-lived. It was around midnight when the winds grew so fierce that the boat began to leap out of the water. They went up to the store and banged on its door. Arnoldo let them in. He was dressed in tiger-striped silk pajamas. Juan looked at Eleanor and winked. He tried to arrange to sleep in Arnoldo's room but ended up in the storage closet cradled on top of coffee bean bags. Eleanor slept in Juanita's room on the floor next to Fabio's cage. The bird sang her a lullaby, "Au Clair de la Lune." And even though the song had a lovely melody and was sung in French, the words *candle* and *flame* were easy to pick out and charged her thoughts with images of Liam's face and the boat aflame. She had a thick rug underneath and a thin coverlet over her. She didn't sleep much. The storm was fierce, and when she did drift off, her dreams tumbled in, haunted by reenactments of the evening's events and awakening her with fright.

The next day, when she woke up, the tension in her body was so tight that she felt like a boa constrictor had her in a death grip. Arnoldo gave her salve from the store to put on her wounds. "That boat beat you up," he had said. She thanked him, acknowledging that putting out fires was a tough job. Exhausted, Eleanor and Juan ate breakfast with Juanita, Fabio, Bob, and Arnoldo. Eleanor found herself fidgeting uncomfortably at the table and unable to eat much. Arnoldo watched and asked her if she had hives, then suggested she smoke some ganja. She took Arnoldo up on his offer. They all had a few hits, except for Juanita, Bob, and Fabio, who left to play outside. The weed made her laugh, and her appetite returned. *Sure,* she said to herself. *Nothing happened.*

Now midday, she lay on a hammock in the sandy backyard of the Beach Lodge. Her thoughts about Liam's death mixed. The evening still preyed upon her emotions. She felt confused about why she had taken the folder in the first place. She sensed Harry to be one of those people who could take care of himself, *no need to pry.* If she had just let the matter go, she and Juan would be on their way to their next stop, a remote island with only a handful of people living on it. Then off to their next stop, the mainland, to gather more mail. It was a simple life. Its lax manner something she would miss if she were eventually hired by a scuba diving school. She also found herself wondering who Liam truly was, because she knew very little about him, except that he was rude, ugly-acting, and possibly insane. During his forty-something years, no doubt he had days of being a better person. If he hadn't died, the chances of him becoming a solid, kind man, she placed at one in a million. Yet, who was she to judge?

It was then that Eleanor became distracted by two beachgoers, Lucy and Freddy. She watched them bumble out of the Lodge and toss their clothes off to reveal bathing suits, as they galumphed to the water's edge. Once in the water, they shouted Liam's name. This had Eleanor sitting up to find out why. They spoke of him being dead. How would they know? An uneasiness ran through her veins. When they made amends for Liam's early death and even piled a bunch of rocks by the water as a memorial, her breathing grew short, and the inklings of an alarm pounded at her stomach and head. "What the...?"

Chapter
22

Nothing Happened

It was late afternoon when Lucy and Freddy woke up from their nap on the beach. Heads hurting and tongues hardened by lack of water, they put their clothes back on their sun-dried bodies and made their way to Milly's.

"I need ice water," Lucy said, drudging her feet along the shell and dirt road.

"Yes, ice would be nice."

Freddy figured they had at least two hours before sunset. They passed the church and observed it was shut down for the day, the desk and chalkboard had been brought back in. The place was stark and lonely looking. "Ghostly," he mumbled. They also saw that the store doors were open and figured Arnoldo had returned. "The mayor's back," Lucy said. "Should we go talk to him?"

"Maybe. Look, Eleanor's at the bar," Freddy said. "Let's question her first."

They paused for a moment to look at Juanita, who was back down on the dock fishing with Bob, while Fabio sang the Beatles song "Yesterday" in his cage.

"How apropos," Lucy said.

They walked into the gin joint and sat down. Milly was in her usual stance, elbows and breasts resting on the counter. She was chatting with Eleanor and Juan, who were at the bar eating. The remnants of rice, beans, and fish were all that was left of their meal; each had a fresh beer in front of them. The brown bottles were beaded with sweat. Eleanor kept her head angled away from Lucy and Freddy. Her bruised hand was down by her side against her thigh. Milly, earlier, had asked her if she needed ice, which she accepted, the coolness a blessed relief. Her excuse: "The fire, and the boat tumbling in the storm, banged me up." Milly's response? To shrug, smile, and display a narrow eye. Eleanor had whispered to Juan that she must know something. Juan didn't seem to notice and spoke of his mother's hernia issues with a lightness that only a guiltless but caring man would possess.

"Milly, could we have ice waters, please?" Freddy said and leaned into the counter for support.

"*Don* with drinking for the day?" She smiled.

"For the time being," Freddy answered. Lucy concurred with a nod.

Milly handed them waters from a cooler located on the floor. "Arnoldo and Dan checked your pool out. No body. You probably imagined it. Well, that's the consensus."

Eleanor's head popped up. Juan reached over and gently touched her hand. She placed the last spoonful of food into her mouth and swallowed hard.

"Interesting," Lucy said and gave Milly a once-over. She gulped half her water, sighed, and gave Eleanor a cryptic squint. "We found Liam in our swimming pool this morning. You wouldn't know anything about that?"

"There's a pool on the island?" Eleanor inquired. From the corner of her eye, she could see Juan smile. Her beer cradled in her hands, she took a swig.

"I have a question," Lucy said, still focused on her. "Do you swim in a bathing suit or underwear? Just an observation."

Eleanor laughed. "Odd thing to ask." She took another swig.

"And?" Freddy interjected.

Eleanor chuckled as if they'd gone off-kilter. Eyebrows arched, head cocked, and with a side glance, she said, "I have a bathing suit, and I wear it."

Freddy gave Lucy a pilito; she tucked it into her shorts' pocket.

A moment of silence came over the place. Juan took a noisy sip of his beer, and Eleanor placed her fork and napkin on her empty plate and handed it to Milly. When Freddy and Lucy began whispering loudly to each other, they drew the bar into their conversation. They wanted to ask Eleanor if she had taken Liam's folder, but they both agreed she probably hadn't killed him since she didn't have a dirt bike or a car.

Milly shrugged, which caused her breasts to wallow back and

forth near a bowl of pretzels. When she stood up to point an angry index finger at Lucy and Freddy, she knocked the bowl off the counter. Ignoring the spill, she scolded, "I told you two. They found nothing. Even walked up and down the beach. No body, no crime. Everyone is innocent. Including you two." Her stern voice stopped Lucy and Freddy from blabbering further. She then bent down and picked up the bowl from the floor.

"Good thing too," Arnoldo said. He swaggered into the bar area; his budgie penis pressed against his left inner thigh, which was different because it was usually against his right. "You two. No more thinking you found a dead body. It's bad for business."

"NO body, NO crime," Milly repeated for the third time, placing the bowl back up on the counter with sandy pretzels in it. She twisted the top off a beer and handed it to Arnoldo. He took it and immediately sucked half down.

"Yah... Just like Milly say. Hell, Danny and I checked everywhere for the guy you two said you saw." Arnoldo paused to belch, then continued. "Even his room at the Beach Lodge is empty. Stuff gone. Must have left on a boat this morning." He finished off the rest of his beer and belched again. His glasses down on his nose, he pushed them up and turned toward Lucy. "Next time I ask you if my daughter took the donkey to school, I expect you to tell the truth."

"I did. When you asked me, they were fishing."

Arnoldo smiled. "Yah, the donkey's good at catching fish." He paused to sigh. He continued with warmth in his eyes: "Fabio told me you brought him mangosteens. Thank you, I like them too. Anyway, yah, that new fellow, the one you thought you saw, left on a boat." He glanced from Lucy to Freddy and back again. "No more discussion. It would be nice, though, if you guys could find some water for the island. My five-star hotel needs it." He walked back to the store.

Eleanor, who listened in disbelief, sat frozen in her seat. Juan once again touched her hand, this time adding a wink. She forced a smile, then glanced over at Milly. Not wanting to appear fazed, she breathed and said, "I was thinking of diving. Do you know if the scuba fellow has evening dives?"

"You need a certificate first or at least to be taking lessons," Lucy said with authority. "I know these things because I help Josey."

Freddy nudged Lucy's knee. "You mean you bother him."

"I have my dive master," Eleanor said. She then dug into her fanny pack and pulled her PADI card out and tossed it on the counter. Lucy picked it up. It said *divemaster*, and on the back was Eleanor's picture. She was smiling, her hair messily pulled into a side ponytail, her green eyes prominent.

"I got it in Panama."

"We're dowsers," Lucy said, a hint of boasting in her tone. "Happy-go-lucky dowsers. Or rather, we were happy-go-lucky, and then we weren't, but now we're back. Right, Freddy?"

"Yes, happy again," Freddy said. "We have jobs. Much too busy to dive," Freddy threw in.

"Josey sometimes dives at night with the lesson folk," Milly said, bringing the conversation back to something concrete. Then she perked up, back stiff, boobs high, and stared off toward the dive shop road. "Well, speak of the devil, he's back from the mainland."

Everyone turned to watch Josey's blond hair disappear behind a thicket of mealy, tall grasses and spindly pine trees.

Lucy immediately nudged Freddy's hip. "You owe me a pilito. He went to get supplies."

"Milly didn't say that."

"What do you think going to the mainland means?"

Freddy handed Lucy another pilito and grumbled, "This is getting expensive." He then leaned toward Lucy's ear and whispered, "Let's go check and see if the body is really gone."

"I suppose, but I don't want to become a suspect again."

"That would be a shame. Okay, if he's there, we can't tell anyone."

"Then what's the point?" Lucy frowned.

"I'm not sure yet," Freddy said, making an *O* mouth.

"I bet he's not there."

"Well, I don't think he is there either, so I'm not betting."

Lucy shrugged. "We should think of another bet."

"Yes, but I don't have one yet."

They asked for two more bottles of water and left.

Eleanor, Milly, and Juan watched them walk down to the main road. They seemed to be arguing. "Those two. My God!" Milly said. "Dead bodies, dowsing. Funny folk."

"Yeah." Eleanor finished off the rest of her beer. Standing up, she paid for Juan and herself. Juan didn't protest.

Juan, having mopped up the last bits of food with his fingers, asked Eleanor, "You stay'n at the lodge tonight?"

"Yup, I got a room. It's simple and has a view of the ocean. I like it."

"I like the coffee bean bags at the store. They smell nice. Last night I dreamed I was swimming in a bowl of java." He then winked at Eleanor again. Milly handed him two unopened beers. He got up and patted Eleanor's shoulder and smiled. "I'm going to see if Arnoldo needs more refreshment."

Eleanor and Milly chuckled. They watched Juan walk over to the store and walk in. Eleanor then looked into Milly's eyes and Milly back at hers. They remained silent and still as though attempting to read each other's thoughts, Eleanor more urgent in her quest. She wanted to know what Milly knew about the death of Liam. And possibly, Milly felt Eleanor should just pretend "nothing happened." Eleanor was unable to assess Milly's thoughts, so she looked at the road to the dive shop. "Well, this day has had its ups and downs," Eleanor eventually said.

"Yah, back up again, eh? Now check the dive shop out. Josey, he's a nice man. But watch yahself. Between Mateo and Josey, those two have had more ass than a toilet." Milly shot Eleanor a smile and went back to gazing at the bay. Eleanor smiled, too. She recalled at the orphanage being warned about Harry and his charm. Could Josey be another Harry? she wondered.

"I think I'll head back to the hammock on the beach and read a little first. It's early, still. Let the food digest before heading over." Eleanor gave Milly a small wave goodbye as she headed off toward the Beach Lodge. Her walk was purposeful yet apprehensive. She felt the death of Liam teetered on the edge of being found out, and "nothing happened." It made her tense, and she could feel her lunch twisting inside her stomach. Then it occurred to her that none of the propri-etors of the island wanted a dead body, let alone a murdered one. It would cause the mainland police to show up followed by damaging rumors and noisy reporters. She smiled, *they've gotten rid of him.* Her head cleared, and her stomach stopped its nonsense. *It never happened.*

Chapter
23

Looking From The Outside In

Lucy and Freddy sat down on a shale boulder near a ledge overlooking the dive shop. They had just returned from Squash Beach and felt tired from the walk and the day's events. Their bodies hunched over, they dangled their legs in the reeds below. From where they sat, they could see Josey on the dock coiling a line. He seemed relaxed, a woman's straw hat on his head; an olive-green T-sheet hung loosely over his beige cargo pants. His feet were bare.

After Josey finished with the line, he unwound a hose and began washing down the deck and the benches of his boat. He then wiped it all dry with a cloth. When he got out of the boat, he dragged a large brown duffel from the cockpit and placed it on the dock. He then got back in, turned the boat on, drove it next to the gas pump, secured the boat against the dock with lines, shut the engine down, and began to pump gas into the tank. "I wonder what's in the duffel?" Lucy said, taking a sip of water. Their headaches and dry mouth were gone, but they were left with the residual effects of feeling out of sorts and fuzzy from the earlier booze. Lucy continued, "Clothes." She then looked at Freddy. "I think I'll sleep well tonight." Then grew excited. "Do you want to bet. I say clothes."

"No, because what else would it be? Oh, maybe supplies. I bet it is supplies."

They shook hands.

Lucy found an orange in her bag, along with several mangosteens hidden in pockets she didn't even know the daypack had. They split the first orange. She handed half of the orange to Freddy by breaking it off with the peel on. She watched him strip the fruit and pop the whole half into his mouth. Juice dripped onto his chin. "Maybe you should splash water on your face," she remarked. Freddy ignored her and wiped the drips off with his hand. Lucy refrained from further comment. Along with not staring at people anymore, she wanted to work on not being a mean girl. With barely a whiff of wind in the air, the evening sun had flattened the sea in front of them. The sky was filled with birds and beetles chattering like experienced gossips. For a while they sat in silence, affected by the tranquility.

Then Freddy spoke: "Yup...yup. No body, no crime," and pointed at a flock of brown pelicans gliding along the ocean's surface. "Isn't that gorgeous?"

"No crime, no guilt," Lucy replied. She noticed the size of Freddy's hand that was now resting on the rock and, unable to help herself, she said, "I bet you're good at opening jars."

"Is that a real bet? I don't know how to make sense of it," Freddy said.

"No, just a way of speaking."

"Well, I'm strong. So, I suppose I am good at opening jars."

Lucy refocused her attention on Josey. "I wonder what he got on the mainland?"

"Spark plugs. A wire." Freddy wiped his brow. "What else do we have to eat?" Lucy dug into her day pack and pulled two mangosteens out. Freddy immediately peeled and ate one. Lucy took her time.

"I never thought the place was seedy; you did. You said the monkeys had issues even though there aren't any monkeys on this island," Lucy remarked and nibbled on her mangosteen.

"Speaking of monkeys, I think he's eating a banana."

Josey had a banana in his hand. He took large bites, which caused his cheeks to puff out. His other hand was still on the pump handle. A pelican landed on a piling by his head, and he appeared to be talking to it with his mouth full.

Freddy shrugged. "Odd man...I'd like a banana. You have any of those sugar bananas?"

"Eaten." Lucy, eyes still on Josey, exhaled a whimsical breath. "There's something about him. I think he's very confident for a shy man."

Freddy looked at Lucy and said, "I don't think he's shy at all. An odd duck like most recluses." He then paused to study her face. "This crush you have on him is annoying."

"I think I just like looking at him."

"I thought you were going to stop that nonsense."

"Seems boring to stop." Lucy shrugged.

"Well, he is good-looking. Not that I notice those things in men. But he'd be dreamier if he didn't dye his hair. It's tacky. I prefer a more natural look."

Lucy looked over at Freddy and laughed, then grew serious. "Do you think I'll ever get that horrible, bloated body of Liam's out of my head?"

"What if it really was just a piece of driftwood? What if we just imagined it was Liam?" he muttered. "No one seems to think anything took place. What I mean is, all this hoopla, for nothing." He then huffed. "I bet he floated away, or Dan and Arnoldo disposed of him. All because of that five-star hotel. I bet it won't even be built."

"That's a lot of bets," Lucy remarked.

"Just a figure of speech."

"Yeah, hard to prove any of it."

"Why if I were a real detective, I'd question the whole lot of them over and over again until they stumbled. But I've given up on that job." Freddy blew out a puff of air. "I'd like dinner. The divers are most likely at the Porch Bar and Grill, swigging down some cold ones by now." Freddy's gaze was now planted on Josey's every move.

"Not yet. It's peaceful here," Lucy said, eyes still on Josey.

Freddy slumped into the rock, while Lucy shifted her position for better comfort. Josey was back on his boat. He was fiddling with the scuba tanks that were secured to the port gunwale. The sun had turned the ocean a pinkish gray and the sky the same color. The lack of light turned Josey into a featureless silhouette. Lucy's and Freddy's bodies softened; their snacks had put them into a lazy stupor. They had the feeling time passed but in slow undisguisable increments. Then unexpectedly, another person appeared on the dock. They perked up and sat forward.

Wearing a raspberry-colored sundress, she had a day pack slung over her shoulder. Her thick dark hair was tied back with a colorful headband. She stopped by the first dock piling to look around. Seeming to spot Josey, she continued down the dock, her flip-flops slapping the clapboards.

"Are you Josey?" she shouted while shielding her eyes from the low sun.

"It's Eleanor," Lucy whispered. "Do you think she's pretty?"

"Now, don't be jealous. If you bothered to get certified, you could dive with him too," Freddy said in a low voice. He then made a deep, muted grunt. "Yes, a very pretty Greek girl."

Lucy smiled. "Here's your chance. Ask her what nationality she is again." She then laughed lightly. "I could use another pilito." She then said, "New bet. I bet she's going to ask for a job."

"She has a job," Freddy replied and turned his focus back toward Lucy.

"Boat's broken," Lucy replied, keeping her gaze on Eleanor.

"Ummm...." Freddy held out his hand. "I bet she's going to ask to go diving."

"She said that is what she wanted to do earlier." Lucy frowned.

"Well, that's my bet," Freddy said triumphantly.

She looked at Freddy and laughed. They shook over the bet, and then both darted their attention back to the dock.

Chapter
24

Eleanor and Harry

Josey stood upright and looked at Eleanor from his boat. "Yes, I'm Josey. What can I do for you?"

Eleanor continued to walk toward him. When he took off his hat and brushed his hair back, she abruptly stopped, and her breath backtracked into her throat. She sputtered, "Oh," and placed both hands over her mouth, then found herself smiling, a big broad smile that burst into a strange, fluttered laugh. Unable to utter a word, she remained stationary, stumped dumb by the man she knew to be Harry.

Josey, with his hands on his hips, looked off toward the ocean, then back again at Eleanor, then off to the sea again. "Is there something wrong?" he asked, looking directly at her, his tone weary and dismissive. It wasn't the reaction she had hoped for. She had dreamt of this moment for a whole year, but now that it had occurred, it was all wrong, deflated and horrible. He didn't recognize her. Liam's death didn't help either. It made her feel awkward and odd. She stood mute and motionless although her whole interior trembled.

Josey stepped out of the boat by using the bench by the gunwale and jumped onto the dock. He was still light on his feet and graceful, she thought, still strong and athletic. "No, nothing's wrong," she finally said and took a few more steps toward him. Maybe he needed glasses. Josey went to do the same but stopped. A glint of recognition crossed his night blue eyes, which cheered her up, and she began to bubble again at being reunited, but then he shook his index finger as though trying to remember something. It occurred to her that he had forgotten her name. Although she often pooh-poohed the relationship as short and long ago, it had also been very intense. The disappointment that she had meant so little to him as to not remember her name crushed her chest, and her heart ached, and her smile vanished. Then a twig snapped up by the shale rock, and Eleanor's attention shot over toward the sound. It was Freddy and Lucy. They were hunched down behind red heliconia flowers. Their eyes and the tops of their heads could be seen through the petals. Before she could wave to them, they disappeared. But she could hear their loud whispers:

"Why would she just say 'oh'? Like he has mud on his face," Freddy questioned.

"I think she saw us."

"We were quick but maybe not quick enough," Freddy muttered.

"It's all very strange. I wonder if they know each other. New bet. I say they know each other."

"How? When? Let me think. Possibly they are both in on the murder of Liam."

"I thought we decided that we made it up," Lucy replied.

"Oh, I forgot. Okay, well, now no more talking...Possibly they met before. Or maybe it's love at first sight," Freddy said.

"Or hate? Why aren't they saying anything?" Lucy queried.

"Shhh...maybe they are but you're talking too much, and I can't hear."

Although Eleanor was slightly amused by their dialogue, the hurt she felt inside, which caused her fingers to tingle and stomach to fold in, made the humor of the busybodies flat and baseless. She looked at Harry. He was now focused on Freddy and Lucy and chuckled, then shook his head, rubbed his forehead, and looked back at Eleanor. He appeared distant. *Possibly because he can't remember who I am,* she thought, *then rethought...it wouldn't even bother him not to know a woman's name.* She began to wonder why she ever liked him. She watched him pick up a wrapper off the gunwale. His reticent behavior, annoying. Did he know she had been part of Liam's murder? Eleanor was under the impression Milly knew, which meant the Aussies, Ernesto, and Arnoldo did too. So, why wouldn't Harry?

Once again, there was a sound from the heliconia flowers. Both Eleanor and Harry looked over. She welcomed the distraction.

"This is very boring. I mean, someone needs to say something." It was Freddy's voice.

"I feel like I'm going to fall asleep," Lucy replied.

Eleanor smiled and went back to her situation, Harry. She should introduce herself and see if her name would ring a bell or, better yet, just leave. Instead of diving and living on the island for a week or two, she would take the ferry back to the mainland and leave Honduras, possibly go to Costa Rica since she'd never been. Her mouth grew cotton-like because the truth was, she didn't want to leave. She cleared her throat and lifted her chin into the air and said, "You're very tan. And the hair, not really your color."

Harry remained silent. His eyes, bright and intense—*hunting prey or hunted*, she thought. *And yup, he has no idea who I am. How brutally awful.* She stood in the low-lying sun beneath the faded blue sky. *Run, Eleanor, run*, she thought and turned to go.

"Don't go," he said. His accent was still an enigma: Spanish, British, Dutch? It was beautiful to hear.

Eleanor turned back around and let her eyes meet his. "If you call me Maddy or Phoebe or—"

"—Eleanor. Of course, it's you. It took me a minute. And well, I... Hell, you see, I have this dream, and you're in it, but you have mud all over you, and well. I just...the shock of seeing you. And..." He brushed his hair back again with his hand. "You look great. Different, though. More grown-up—"

"—I'm a year older," she said, cutting him off.

"A whole year. I guess that makes me a year older too." He chuckled and walked over but stopped a foot away. "I'm sorry for how we left it. Bit of a blur. Bumped into Alex in Tegucigalpa. He told me you went off with some fellow in a sailboat. I hope that was good... I mean. Hell."

"For a while," she said, then thought about what Alex had said. He had lied to Liam and the minister. Alex and Harry had been in the city together.

Harry let his arm swing out and bashfully touched her arm, then let it slip to her hand. She winced when he squeezed her bruised knuckles. "What do we have here?" He inquired. He gently held her

217

hand and examined the damage. "Boxing lately?" When he looked at her face he frowned. "I guess so. I have ice. Do you need ice?" He made a motion as though to leave and get some. He seemed nervous to her, something new. She had always known him as a stalwart of confidence, to the point of being overly cavalier.

"No, it's okay. I'm fine," she said. She wanted to make a joke, like, "you should see the other guy," but didn't think it funny.

He stepped in and hugged her. His body was warm and smelled of salt, sweat, and sea, with an essence of myrrh. She hugged him back. A tight, strong hug. When they let go, they moved a couple of feet away from each other. But he leaned in again and touched her cheek and peered at her lip and the bruise on her chin with concern. "No worries," she said. "We had a fire on the boat. I bumped into a few walls. Not a big deal."

"What boat?" He seemed puzzled.

"The mail boat."

"Mail boat?"

"My job. I help the Honduran government deliver the mail," she said proudly with a spark of mirth. She thought the job rather peculiar to have and assumed Harry would too.

"You're the one." He looked up at the heliconia flowers. He could see the tops of Lucy's and Freddy's heads. "They're spying on us."

Eleanor looked over too. "I know."

"So, you're the mail lady. I thought you'd just arrived... A tourist." He drew his eyes away from the flower bed and refocused them on Eleanor. His eyes were clear and bright and resembled the color of a New England ocean on a wintery day. His brow furrowed; his cheeks bulged as he swished his tongue over his teeth. "Hell. I..." He looked over toward Lucy and Freddy again, then back at Eleanor and leaned into her to whisper, "Thank you." He lingered by her ear, and she could feel his lips desiring to say more but stuck somewhere in mid-play, his breath warm and sweet. She stepped back, the heat of the moment too much.

Harry looked off at the sea and back at her. In a low voice, he said, "I believe we need to talk. But those two hiding in the flowers..." And then he paused and changed the subject. "You know, the boys...uh, Mateo, Arnoldo, Dan...have spoken about you for months."

Eleanor frowned.

"In a good way." He then chuckled. "Unbelievable. All this time, you've been coming to the island, and we never bumped into each other." He rambled. *Flustered or just surprised?* she wondered.

"*Parajo hermoso*—your nickname," he said and gave an embarrassed chuckle. "The boys said you kept to yourself, quiet, a *beautiful bird* moving across the ocean free." His eyes bore into her, then twinkled, and he chuckled again. "And all this time it's been you."

"Ships crossing but never meeting." Eleanor felt confused, flattered on one hand that she had a pretty nickname but not happy to be talked about. She looked around because she wasn't sure what next to say. The brown duffel on the dock by the boat caught her attention. She recalled the last time she had seen it. It had been full of money. Harry followed her gaze, and said, "I'm like a pregnant woman. A packed bag for the dash-off. But fate has been kind to me lately, and I think I'll stay put." He gave her an endearing smile; one she had seen time and time again when he'd entered their room or saw her on the beach or in the cafeteria while at the orphanage.

"Josey Wales. You like those bad-boy names. I prefer Harr—"

"Josey," he said, quickly correcting her.

"A little difficult. But yes, Josey. Well, I was going to ask you about diving tonight," she spoke. Although happy he did know who she was, she still felt disconcerted by his presence and the circumstances surrounding it. "I rather not dive."

Once again, they were interrupted by rustling. This time near the end of the dock behind a large barrel for trash, they could see Lucy's arm protruding from one side and Freddy's arm on the other.

"They're behind the barrel now," Josey said, amused.

They could hear Lucy and Freddy argue:

"You need to move behind me. Your arm is sticking out."

"You move behind me."

"Then I can't see."

"Lucy! Freddy! What are you doing?" Harry shouted at them.

They both stood up.

"Throwing away garbage," Lucy said and tossed the orange and mangosteen rinds into the barrel.

"Is Harr a nickname? Freddy asked.

"No," Josey replied.

"You owe me a pilito," Lucy said.

"I bet she wanted to go diving, so we're even," Freddy barked at

Lucy. Lucy had her hands folded over her chest. "I don't owe you a pilito," she said in a harsh tone to Freddy. "You said she'd ask to go diving. But she said she wanted to go diving."

"What's the difference?" Freddy said with an incredulous tone.

"There's a difference." Lucy pouted.

Eleanor and Harry looked at each other and laughed. Harry put his index finger in the air, as if to say wait a minute, and inquired, "Hey, did you find water yet?"

"Not yet, but we're on it," Freddy yelled back.

"Why don't you come say hello," he shouted.

"Thank you, but we're busy," Freddy yelled.

"I want to go over and ask them how they know each other, or is it love or hate at first sight," Lucy insisted.

"I want to go eat."

Lucy made a *humph* noise. "Okay, I bet dinner is conch soup."

"I say it's fish stew again."

They shook.

"Before we leave, should we ask them if they knew each other?" Lucy said.

"I'm tired and hungry; let's ask them tomorrow."

"Shame." Then Lucy smiled. "If we find water for the five-star hotel, I bet we can be part owners."

"That's random but fun sounding."

Eleanor and Harry watched them walk away. In mid-step, Freddy and Lucy turned and waved goodbye. They waved back.

"I think they call themselves the happy-go-luckies," Harry said, then raised an eyebrow at Eleanor. His face turned serious. Then a board creaked by the shop, and they both looked over. It was Mateo.

"Hey, boss. The divers will be here soon. Shall I fill the boat?" He had the same girly straw hat on that Harry wore. Eleanor smiled.

"Done," Harry said.

"Okay." He swirled around and headed into the shop.

Eleanor cleared her throat. "Do you like bacon?"

"Who doesn't?"

"Tomorrow's Bacon Tuesday."

He nodded. His eyes seemed to question where her line of thought was going.

"Meet me tomorrow at the No Name. Early, when it first opens," she said.

He rubbed his chin. "I think what we need to talk about requires privacy."

"We'll sit on the beach. Away from the crowd." She then leaned in and whispered. "We can talk or just eat bacon." Her eyes were warm. She wasn't sure if she wanted to know any more about his past doings because she wasn't sure if the information would be troubling or positive. What she had known of him was that he was a kind person. A fun man to be with that bounced children on his knees and bought fruit for her when he went into town. It felt good to see him. More than good. It felt wonderful, invigorating and explosive. She wasn't ready yet to ruin it with the truth. She didn't want to tell him about Dorian, either. And Liam wasn't a subject she was comfortable with. Overall, she felt secrets were okay to have and preferred to hear about his life at the present time or before all the trouble started. *That would be safe territory*, she thought. And she would tell him about Panama.

Harry remained quietly thinking. He then cleared his throat and sighed. "I never go there, but I'll make an exception for you."

Eleanor beamed and took his hand and squeezed it, then walked away. She could feel him watch her as she made her way down the dock. She knew she looked good. She knew she exuded an air of assurance, even when it wasn't there. Her childish, thin figure had filled out over the year, and the woman inside of her ripened. She maneuvered up the grassy incline to the path, her dark hair swaying with each step, and disappeared behind spindly pines, thistle bushes, and sage.

Chapter
25

Bacon Tuesday

Lucy and Freddy stood outside the No Name restaurant with Arnoldo, Juanita, Bob, Milly, Juan, Aurora, Dan, and Mateo. They were waiting for Lilly to open the restaurant door. It was early morning, and sleep was still visible on their faces: puffy eyes, the sandman work not cleared from the corners of Freddy's, whereas Lucy, Arnoldo, and Bob kept yawning. It seemed no one had the energy to speak. Instead, they seemed to find comfort in staring at Eleanor and Josey, who sat on the beach by the water's edge. It was another humid morning without wind, their skin damp, and their stomachs growled. Then Juan sighed, which unhinged a deluge of nonchalant comments from the group.

"Do you think the hairy man will cook the bacon crispy?" Arnoldo spoke.

"I like it chewy," Milly mewed. The group looked at her in disgust.

"I think they like each other," Lucy said, pointing her chin at Eleanor and Josey.

"They'll be fine if she leaves in a few days," Mateo smirked. "No sense trying to change that man."

"We're building a five-star hotel. Why would anyone leave?" Juan interjected, smiling at Arnoldo. "My mother will love it."

"I think the spring is under the ground, an aquifer." Freddy's voice raspy, he cleared his throat and went over to a bush to expel the phlegm. This caused Lucy to look at him and make a face. He walked back over and pointed his finger at the earth. "If we dig a hole, we'll have water."

Lucy then smiled at Freddy. "Gosh, Freddy, aren't you smart this morning. A little gross but smart." Freddy smiled back at her. Their eyes remained entwined for a few minutes more than necessary, which caused them to stand unusually close to each other. Lucy giggled. "Just think, when we get hot from digging, we can swim in our pool."

"You're digging too, I bet you won't last." Freddy grinned, holding out his hand.

"I bet I last longer than you." They shook. Then Lucy looked at Arnoldo. "Once it's built, I'm going to make money having Fabio say the guests' names."

"I'll be the banana holder," Freddy piped in.

"Sounds good, but you might want to ask Fabio first," Arnoldo quipped.

Dan burst out laughing. "We need money, folks, money to build a hotel. I don't suppose one of you has any."

All eight of them looked at Josey sitting beside Eleanor. Juan sighed, then said, "Do you think we can convince him?"

Arnoldo tipped his sunglasses down his nose; his eyes twinkled. "I think so."

The group remained staring at Eleanor and Josey, who were laughing, talking, and digging their toes into the sand. It was then that a sleek-looking sailboat appeared in the bay. It was motoring swiftly with its sails down. The hull was the color of a dark night. The man standing behind the helm wore a baby-blue collared T-shirt and khakis. He was blond and his free hand was on his hip. The group watched him disappear around the bend.

"Must have heard about my Bacon Tuesdays," Lilly said, standing behind the group. Everyone turned and looked at Lilly, who was staring off at the bay. "Now, why are they arguing?" Eleanor and Josey were standing and appeared to be having a disagreement. Josey kept throwing his hands in the air, and Eleanor was pointing at the bay shaking her head. Then abruptly they ran off toward the main road away from the restaurant and disappeared behind a cluster of coconut palms. "Possibly make-up sex." Lilly chuckled. The rest of the group either smiled or chuckled too. "Come on, folks, we're open."

Lucy whispered to Freddy, "I think I know that boat. If it's the same one my friends and I sailed around on, the owner's a cad."

Freddy pondered what Lucy had said, then swished his tongue around his mouth, "Lucy, you seemed to have led a devilish life before coming here."

She nudged him and pouted. "Hardly."

All eight piled into the restaurant. In one of the corners of the restaurant, they pushed together tables and chairs. As they sat waiting for service, they watched the divers come in one by one. First the Italians, then the Irish, and lastly with her dog, the French woman. Lilly's sisters were taking orders, and Ernesto was pouring coffee and milk, while the brother cooked. Because everyone ordered at the same time, the food took longer than usual to prepare. The delivery of the meals was random, for example, one person at a table would receive food and then another at another table, even though everyone had ordered the same thing: bacon, scrambled eggs with cheese, fruit, and pan de coco.

A half-hour passed, and everyone was finally eating if not finished, which was when a stranger walked into the restaurant. He was well built, handsome, tan, blond, and wearing a baby-blue collared shirt and khakis. Lucy caught sight of him and squinted. "Yup, that's him," she mumbled to Freddy.

The blond looked around the restaurant. Spotting a table in the back, he began to walk toward it. Arnoldo stopped him by asking, "Was that your sailboat we saw?"

"She's a beaut, isn't she?" he said, glancing over the folks at the table. He cocked his head to the side when he saw Lucy. "Do I know you?"

"Maybe," she replied, then added. "No."

It was then that Ernesto came by with coffee and milk. He poured the man a mug full and refilled others who wanted more. The man sipped his beverage and was about to walk away when Milly spoke up, "Would you like to sit with us?"

"Yes, thank you. I'm Dori, Dori Titlemen," he said and sat down between Freddy and Dan. They all made introductions, and Dori ordered food from one of Lilly's sisters. The conversation between them started off light and casual. Juan wanted to know how the seas looked today, and Dan was interested in the weather on the mainland since he'd heard it was raining. When Dori's food arrived, he ate a few bites but then leaned back and cleared his throat. "I have a question to ask you all. I got a call from relatives telling me my brother might be here. His name is Liam. Liam Ramos, or I think he's using Titlemen. Grammy's name, I like the sound of it, don't you?"

Everyone sunk deep into their seats, except for Lucy, who frowned, and her face paled. She glanced at Freddy, who appeared puzzled and nauseated. No one spoke, then Dan made a growling noise and waved Lilly over. "Check, please."

The silence spread throughout the restaurant like a distorted, tetchy wave. The quiet in the room was thick as water and just as suffocating. It was then the Irish woman spoke. "There was a drunk man here said to be called Liam. It was rumored he picked up and left on the first ferry out, and then there are the fun rumors. You know, like he fell off the dock and ended up in a tidal pool at Squash Beach half eaten by sharks. Then the sharks dove into the pool and ate him all up." Lucy caught the woman's eye. "Yes, dear, the island is small. Kinda like a toothpick box. Not one person doesn't know about this occurrence. I also heard—"

"—Darling, it's the man's brother," the Irish man said, his expression worried.

The French woman's dog began to bark, and she hushed him. "I have on good authority that he *waz* on the ferry to Roatan. I would check that island. Big, big drunk that *brozer* of yours. When you find him, put him in rehab."

"Ernesto!" Aurora shouted at the innkeeper, who was making more coffee. "Didn't you say you saw him leave on a fishing boat?"

"Yup, got on one of the mainlander's fishing boats. It was early morning. Don't know which way it was going, but possibly to South

America. Those boats go far." He threw his free hand in the air and walked into the kitchen.

The Italian boy who spoke English leaned in, "*Iya* saw him row *awaya* in a tiny little *boata*."

Dori's eyes followed each person's story with confusion and concern. "Good lord...possibly my brother. What did the fellow look like?" Everyone looked at Lucy to describe him. She sputtered, then spoke, "Tall, didn't tan well, lipless."

"Oh dear, yes...that definitely could be him. But which story is correct?" Dori's nervous eyes studied Lucy as though she would know the truth. The rest of the group seemed to be holding their breath. Then Lucy looked at Freddy. He raised his brow and shrugged as if to say, 'you choose which story.'

Wide-eyed and hesitant at first, she began, "Well, at first, the tidal pool story...and...and..." She stopped there and looked at Freddy again. He, too, looked like he was holding his breath now. Lucy twisted, then shrugged, "Well, it seems the shark rumor was because a piece of driftwood got into Freddy's and my pool. And...well, creepy driftwood, and you know, it caused the bad rumor. But I bet...I bet he took the little *boata*. I like that. I think he took a little *boata* somewhere fun. Isn't that a nice story?"

"I'm not looking for nice. I'm looking for what really happened." Dori scratched his head and let his eyes trail over the faces of everyone. A few had gone back to eating. Then the chatter started up again. The table of future hotel owners remained quiet for a few minutes more, then they, too, began to eat and talk to each other. Dori, seeing that no one had anything more to say, munched on a piece of bacon. Placing the half-eaten piece on his plate, he spoke loudly: "A tidal pool, a fishing boat, a ferry, a rowboat, South America?" His last few words were filled with doubt, his tone trailing off and weary.

"Fishing boat," Freddy said.

Lucy twisted for a minute, then a sly expression crossed her face. "*Boata.*"

"Is there anyone else on this island I could question?" Dori sighed.

Mateo rose and looked at the divers. "Let's get going, folks."

The Irish were already paying their bill and looked at Dori. The woman smiled. "We're heading over to the dive shop to take our PADI exam." She looked at the French woman and the Italians and said, "Come on, we need to get a move on," then looked back to Dori and said, "We're being tested in the water today, and we also need to take the written part... I hope my memory doesn't fail me. It's all very exciting. Why don't you walk over with us? You can ask Josey if he knows anything and possibly that woman...I think a mail lady... might be with him. She should know a thing or two."

Arnoldo, who had been listening to the conversation, jumped up. He knocked over his chair and jiggled the table. His eyes were wild and darted around. Then he focused on his breakfast companions, who remained silent with questioning looks and fidgety hands. He mumbled, "The hotel. Must save the hotel." They all sighed a sound of relief, except for Lucy and Freddy, who looked at each other, confused.

Arnoldo skirted out from the table. With his long legs, he took big strides brushing by the divers and Dori and went out the door lickety-split. His abrupt exit had everyone wondering where he had gone off to. A few seconds went by, then the only sounds to be heard were the high-pitched whine of a dirt bike engine being pushed faster and faster toward the leeward side of the island, and the rhythmic rumble of the ocean's waves as they pushed and pulled at the shore.

Acknowledgement

I would like to thank the members of the Westport Rivers Writers Guild: Corey, Paull, Jerome, and Dwayne. They patiently, and at times, not so patiently, listened to the first draft and some of the second draft of this novel. The Guild was and is very instrumental in keeping me writing. Thank you to my partner, Paul Andonian, for letting me read bits and pieces to him at breakfast, lunch, and dinner. A great big thank you to all the Beta Readers, proofreaders, and to editors.

L. Wendell Vaughan has written for various magazines and newspapers. Rabbits and Moons is her first full length novel, published in 2020. She wrote a children's book in 2001 called "Andy Ant, What Could Possibly Be On The Other Side to See?' The book has been noted for its lessons on diversity and making new friends, and was made into a play by the Circle Nursery School. Vaughan, a world traveler, has spent a vast amount of time in Mexico, Central and South America. She taught high school history and English for 21 years and lives in the southeast area of Massachusetts with her partner, Paul, and her horse, Pages.

Made in the USA
Middletown, DE
04 August 2023

35823781R00139